For my best friends,

Who I have unashamedly mocked, ripped off and repackaged for the sake of a good story.

For London,

The city that emotionally and financially ruined me in the best possible way.

And...

For Will Smith,

Listen, you're a really lovely guy and I have always fully supported you and your endeavours (even after *Wild Wild West* which was a complete disaster of a movie!) BUT I'm gay.

So I think we should just be friends. Soz.

Chapter One

I would buy the milk myself. There was no point placing false hope in my elusive flat mate to do it. So I shoved my feet into my battered trainers, grabbed the front door key and headed to the shop at the bottom of my road. It was raining heavily but I refused to wear a coat, not because I loved the sensation of sideways rain on my skin but because right there and then my mind was occupied with something bigger. Instead I pretended my hoodie was magically waterproof. It wasn't, at all. Not even a little bit. My soaked T-shirt was irritating my chest, and I scratched at the saturated cotton. Hugging myself, I dodged the puddles with their floating cigarette butts, as though that would make a difference.

Refusing a carrier bag was another big mistake. Huge. I'm a massive advocate for saving the planet but not when I'm trying to open the front door with a carton of milk in one hand and my mobile phone ringing to the tune of *Sexual Healing* in the other. The ringtone was hilarious two weeks ago but today I wanted my 99p back. I had just missed a call from Jason. Odd. He never really called me, except for when he was drunk and trying to convince me to have sex with him. It was just harmless tomfoolery, because he knew there wasn't a hope in hell I would ever let his penis anywhere near me.

Closing the fridge door and kicking off my trainers into the hall, I dialled Jason's number. I would simply get this last call out of the way and then pick up from where I had left off. He answered instantly, so I knew something was very wrong. I ignored my instincts and laughed down the phone, expecting to be confronted with incomprehensible slurring and explicit instructions detailing how to find a woman's G spot as he tried to navigate his way home. But this time he was much more subdued. He was certainly drunk but not boisterous or trying to barter with a shopkeeper for a packet of cigarettes he was too smashed to smoke. There was a long pause and I assumed the line had gone dead. Jason interrupted the silence with, "Sam, I need to see you. My dad died this morning."

I didn't know if it was a nervous kind of thing or an insensitive asshole kind of thing, but I often laugh at heartbreakingly tragic moments. A situation could scream the exact opposite of hilarity, but I seemed compelled to giggle or to make highly inappropriate comments. One of my best friends had just told me his father had passed away and I was chuckling as if the awkward silence was the punch line. What a dickhead. Another fine example of why I was heading straight to hell. Screw it. At that stage in my life being a bit of a dick was just a case of go hard or go home.

I composed myself for just long enough to ask Jason where he was. He was calling from a bar the other side of town and I had about twenty-five minutes to get my shit together before I missed the last train. No time to change. What I was wearing would have to do. This was an emergency and I was pretty sure my T-shirt with a hologram of a bikini-clad woman on the front would be fine. I clocked myself in the mirror in the hallway and tried to rearrange the shape of my Afro. My eyes fell down to my T-shirt again. Better zip up my hoodie just to be safe. It was a Sunday after all, so Jesus was probably lurking somewhere, judging me.

I love living in the suburbs, but damn living in the suburbs at the weekend, with no direct Tube line into town. The whole point of moving south of the river from the attention-seeking East End was to experience the leafy streets, the beautiful, expansive parks right on my doorstep. I wanted to be able to go for bike rides without feeling like I was entering a suicide pact with the rest of London's cyclists. And the big city was still just a fifteen-minute train journey away. Today, however, the journey was a little more complicated trying to run for a train when I never run for anything. Life was already far too fast. Slow and steady is how I liked it. I jumped the last four steps descending from the station's pedestrian bridge and threw myself breathlessly into the carriage. My acrobatics were entirely unnecessary as the train continued to sit at the platform for a further five minutes.

I stood for a moment, trying to discreetly stretch my groin after my impressive display of athleticism, and then hobbled to the nearest seat. Pulling out my phone I instinctively began to text my flat mate, Owen, *Bad news with Jason. His dad has died :(On way to see him now in town. I bought some milk.* I then flicked my phone onto silent, as nobody needed to hear my *Sexual Healing* ringtone.

Owen had met Jason only once and I think once was quite enough. It was a night spent drinking and dancing in the living room until 5 a.m. A quiet Tuesday evening that had spiralled into a session of male bonding over sweet and sour chicken balls and copious cans of cider. I was drifting in and out of sleep in the next room and by 1 a.m. I was furious because they were so loud and I had work in the morning. But I was envious, too, because they seemed to be having so much fun. Either way, my cries of "Shut the fuck up for the love of all things decent and holy!" fell on deaf ears.

Owen didn't usually have time for my friends, who would often visit me/use our flat as a youth hostel when passing through London, but he had a lot of time for Jason. Jason would like to think that was because they had a funny-lad-banter connection, but it was mainly down to how his arse looked in the pale blue skinny jeans he wore that night.

"Owen, my love, he's straight," I said.

But Owen just smiled and tilted his head slightly. "Not in those jeans, he's not."

Before I had a chance to put my phone back in my front pocket it vibrated way too loudly to be considered "silent". It was Owen.

"Shit. That's awful. I'm already in town, just finishing work. Let me know what happens. I'll come and meet you if you need me."

I smiled. The boy refused to buy essential groceries but he was always Mister Reliable when you needed him.

The train doors snapped shut. I hadn't thought things through since talking with Jason. I had no idea what I would say to him. He was one of my best friends but our relationship was based on rude jokes and drinking until we fell over. We were not the deep and meaningful kind of buddies who went around singing kum ba yah and talking about our emotions. But I was going to have to do just that. Shit. I fumbled at my phone and googled *bereavement*, but the page wouldn't load as the train headed through a tunnel. I was going to have to wing this meeting and pray that I didn't get it wrong. But I was 90 per cent sure I would get it wrong, and was relying on alcohol for the remaining 10 per cent.

Chapter Two

It wasn't so much that I hated people. I mostly just hated the slow-walking morons who felt the need to suddenly stop in front of me and then expected me to apologise when I bumped into them. Perhaps screaming "I hate people!" as I scuttled away from the man with an oversized suitcase may have been a little dramatic, but for the love of God, MOVE! London Bridge station in rush hour is usually populated by young professionals who think they have the right of way just because they're in a suit, power walking and clutching a coffee cup in one hand and a gym bag in the other. But on a Sunday night it was just young families who had been out for the day and loved-up couples. Bleary-eyed, loved-up couples who got shit faced at lunchtime and were now passionately, but somewhat grotesquely, kissing on a platform. Everyone was heading home for the evening, catching the last overland train, and I was going against the grain, trying to get into the city before the Tube closed.

I hoped Jason was still in the bar and hadn't become restless and moved on. I didn't fancy playing a game of hide-and-seek across a series of drinking holes in the West End. I'd call him when I got near and then take it from there. Jason. Poor Jason. My stomach flipped at the thought of what I might walk into when I met him.

I always enjoy taking my time on the escalators down to the Underground. I stare at all the posters advertising the latest West End shows and at people too, hoping to catch a stranger's eye. I like flashing a grin at strangers and surprising them with unexpected kindness. It's never a sinister smile and I make sure to sparkle my friendly eyes rather than my come-to-bed eyes or my I-have-a-body-in-the-basement eyes. I find that people sometimes struggle with the concept of getting something for nothing and in this case it was a free smile and a knowing nod. Or maybe it was just the idea that I was intruding on their day that made them feel uncomfortable. I like to confuse people with friendliness and a look that says, "Hey, how's it going? I've noticed you today" and then unintentionally make it awkward for both of us. It's like saying "I love you" to someone who already knows you love them but who doesn't hear it nearly often enough. I find that the best reason to do something is simply just because. I guess it's a kind of weird hobby of mine, but I enjoy tripping people up with affection.

That night, however, there was no time for breezy people-watching as I flew down the escalators ignoring everything and everyone. I fixed my eyes directly on the steps in front, still petrified that my foot might get sucked into the sides like the terrifying 1980s public-safety adverts. The image of the shiny Wellington boot being crushed under the motorised steps still haunted me. Finally on the Tube, I was able to relax a little before I changed lines at Bank. I'd be with Jason in twenty minutes.

Still unsure what my plan of action would be if Jason had gone AWOL, I nervously groped for my phone in my jeans pocket. I knew there was no signal but I needed to fiddle with something. It was a bad habit of mine that I had no desire to break. The carriage was half empty, and instead of making up ridiculous stories about how I had been caught up in a zombie apocalypse at an abandoned train station, I rehearsed my words of condolence. My mouth was dry. I ran my tongue over my chapped lips and then exhaled at the thought of a double vodka and Coke.

I used to hate alcohol. I was the kind of kid who would say, "I don't need to get drunk to have a good time!" Yes, I was that kid who had morals in all the right places, until I got horrendously drunk at my friend's seventeenth birthday party. I couldn't even blame peer pressure as my friends had already been drinking for years. That night of overindulgence, broken promises and low standards was instigated by me, myself and I. And of course, like most first-time teenage experiences, it was terrible. I remember thinking that if I focused on a particular spot of my friend's mother's patterned carpet, I could will the room to stop spinning. I couldn't. The situation was made worse by the chocolate cake someone was enthusiastically waving in front of my face, trying to force-feed me in an effort to sober me up. That someone was Jason.

My journey from my wasted youth to my mid-twenties consisted of radioactive alcopops, strange Duty Free liquors from holidays and cocktails with varying degrees of fruity decoration hanging from the side of the glass. When I hit twenty-four I finally settled on a more grown-up tipple – vodka. If I drank enough, it tasted like love. The fact that I would use anything as a mixer, including vodka, exposed my weakness of still acting like a seventeen-year-old with no ambition to grow up anytime soon.

I swiped my Oyster card and passed through the barriers. For a moment I completely forgot my purpose. It was as if I had just woken up from a deep and unintended afternoon nap and had no idea or recollection of how I ended up on the sofa.

Jason. I had to call him now.

When I left my hometown of fresh air, green fields and busybody Neighbourhood Watch for the bright lights of London, I was gripped with a fear that everyone would try to rob me. I would always stand to the side of a street, away from the crowds, clutching my phone for dear life. Six years later I had yet to be mugged, so clearly my crime-prevention technique was working. I left the artificial light of the Tube station and huddled under the archway of a small Italian restaurant. The *Closed* sign was hanging at an angle inside the door but the lights were still on. I dialled Jason's number and it rang out. "For heavens to Betsy!" I exclaimed. I loved that phrase. It was ridiculous and it made no sense, but it reminded me of my mother. Why the hell was Jason not picking up? He knew to expect me. I tried again and looked at my watch like a Parisian mime artist trying to act out the gesture of waiting for someone. My dramatic movement was pointless, as I didn't have an audience. I hit redial and, after the third ring Jason picked up.

"Oh, hi! How are you doing?" His voice was empty and the question was entirely rhetorical. His stable-sounding manner threw me, and instead of getting straight to the point, I played along, unsure of what was happening.

"I'm OK. Just made it. It's stopped raining, so that's nice!"

There was a pause and in that split second my brain shunted back to the reason I had dashed into town dressed like a damp hobo.

"So where are you? Still at our local?" Thank God he was still there. I could hear the video jukebox in the background. "Stay put. I'll be there in five minutes."

Jason mumbled an OK just as I walked away from the Italian restaurant.

The reason the bar had became our local despite the fact that it was miles from where either of us lived, was threefold. One, it was the only place we knew that was open past midnight on a Sunday. Two, the prices were semi-reasonable for London. And most importantly, number three – we liked the name. *The Cellar Door* reminded us of the eighties children's TV programme *Trap Door*. The first time we drank in there we sang the theme tune for the entire day: *"Don't you open that TRAP DOOOOOR!"* We substituted *cellar door* for *trap door* of course. It was also 2 p.m. on a Saturday and we had already sunk three bottles of wine, much to the delight of the other patrons. Oh the hilarity of our combined churlishness! We were supposed to have a cultural day in the city, visiting museums and critiquing a new art exhibition. I was keen to engage in pretentious discussions on brushstrokes reminiscent of the Pre-Raphaelite artists and suchlike, But we both lacked focus and instead we headed towards Soho for liquid inspiration. This was the first time Jason tried to woo me with his drunken affections. It was also the first time of many that I laughed hysterically at his efforts.

Jason and I connected on a fun level. We encouraged each other to be as big, loud and wild as possible just because we knew we could get away with it. We were rarely supervised by sensible friends who would rein us in or talk us out of a truly bad idea. And we thrived on our freedom. Our friendship worked because there was no judgement or weighing up of the pros and cons. Jason was my go-to guy when I needed to justify my nomadic lifestyle. I could unleash my middle-finger attitude, and he would see it and raise me a giant fuck-you in return. We facilitated each other's tendency to be irresponsible clowns without having to apologise for our behaviour. Thought-provoking chats were left at the door or laughed out of the conversation. We had been party pals since we were seventeen. Nothing more and nothing less. So why did he choose to call me on night that was so horrendously serious? Why did he need to see me? I was convinced that nobody really needed me. But here I was, standing at the entrance to The Cellar Door, inhaling short sharp breaths at the prospect of what lay ahead. I had to be the best friend possible right now and not screw this up. I looked down at my digital watch; it read 11:46 p.m. It was the beginning of a long night.

Chapter Three

Jason was hidden away in the far corner of the bar, two tables back from our usual seats. A middle-aged couple occupied them and it really pissed me off. There's a whole damn bar and tonight of all nights they chose our seats! How very dare they. Jason didn't look up as I walked over, and when I neared the table I didn't even hug him; I just swiftly sat down opposite. Even though the video jukebox was playing in the background, Jason had his iPod on and his earphones in. On the table were a torn beer mat and the remnants of a label he must've ripped off a cider bottle. Now he was holding a short glass with a dark, dusty-coloured drink, filled to the top with ice. When I sat down he looked up with his bloodshot eyes, removed his earphones and smiled in acknowledgement of my presence. But it wasn't his usual goofy grin.

"So some schmucks took our seats!" I remarked in a voice that was far too animated and squeaky.

"I know. I was thinking of throwing a beer mat at their heads but I'm not drunk enough." Jason was lying. He was definitely drunk enough; his eyes kept losing focus. But he was the wrong sort of intoxicated. There was no mischievous bounce to his drunken vibe, as it was smothered with a thick layer of sadness. I smiled and moved my hand across the table to hold his. "Then let's get drunk enough!" I said, and he returned my smile.

"I'm going to get a vodka. What are you drinking?" I asked, shuffling out of my seat.

Jason swirled the contents of his glass around and said, "A double whiskey with ice."

I nodded as I left my chair and headed to the bar. The girl behind the bar was new and she fumbled with the till and drink optics. I gave her a reassuring smile and a few "don't worry about its" when she asked me for a third time if it was vodka I'd ordered. She had a rich bronze colour to her complexion that looked far too natural and healthy to be the result of a two-week holiday in Tenerife with excessive use of baby oil and no regard for sun damage. She handed me the drinks, looked over my shoulder and said, "Is your friend okay?" Her accent was soft and melodious, could've been anywhere from French to Italian to Lebanese. It was anglicised but it definitely wasn't English. I was shit at identifying foreign accents but I loved hearing them.

"Define *okay*."

The girl looked at me, puzzled, and I broke her confusion with another smile. "He'll be okay," I said quickly and then turned to head back to the table.

I handed Jason his drink and took a huge gulp of mine. Asking someone if they are okay after they've lost a loved one has to be the most ridiculous question in the world, but there I was about to ask just that. Before the words left my lips he interrupted my thoughts.

"Before you ask, I'm not okay. I feel atrocious but I'm too angry to cry again. I just need to forget for one night. So please let's do just that."

I sat there feeling as useful as a discoloured doily, but I had to respect his wishes. Up until this point I had no idea how his father died but I wasn't going to ask any questions. This is why Jason called me. He didn't want any soul-searching conversations; he just wanted to drown in the unpredictability of alcohol and bring me along for the ride. This night had "head-on collision with a faulty airbag" written all over it, but I was prepared to go with it.

Jason lurched towards me and roughly stuffed one of the ear buds of his iPod into my ear canal.

"I really like the lyrics of this song. I'm thinking of playing it at the funeral," he said, over-enunciating over the noise of the music. After telling me he didn't want to talk about his dad, referencing funeral songs was a pretty poor attempt to change the subject. I smiled awkwardly as he stared at me, awaiting my feedback on the song. I already knew the track; it was one of my favourites –, "Oxygen" by Willy Mason. I loved it, especially the lyrics, but in the space of ten seconds Jason had now singlehandedly ruined it for me. My happy inspirational song was now a song of death to be played during funeral processions. What a prick. As awful and insensitive as it was to feel annoyance towards my grieving friend, I still managed it. I clearly was a bigger prick.

"This is one of my favourite songs," I said and handed back the earphone while taking another slurp of my drink. Jason put both earphones back in and closed his eyes. The entire arrangement was beyond strange. I was sitting in silence across the table from my friend whose dad had just died from causes unknown, watching him listen to his iPod while I searched for divine intervention at the bottom of my vodka and Coke. I pulled out my phone. Resting on the screen was a text from Owen: *Where are you?* It was delivered five minutes ago.

I'm in our local. It's an odd one. Need back up. Bring your drinking hat if you fancy getting involved, I replied. Jason was still listening to his iPod, staring inanely at his glass of whiskey. Owen's reply was swift and comforting: *I'm on my way. See you in 10.*

Owen and I met at university but it wasn't until we were brought together by lack of student-accommodation options that we became friends. It's funny how the prospect of homelessness can accelerate a new friendship. My roommate and I needed another person to live with, so after an awkward chat with Owen ("Hi. We kind of know each other, but not really. Will you live with me?") our friendship began. Five years later and we couldn't live with or without each other. He was my "husband" but without the sex, so exactly like a traditional marriage. Owen was a permanent fixture in my life whether I liked it or not. He was the only person to put up with my shit, see through my shit and actually give a shit at the same time. Sometimes I would forget this and curse out loud at his inability to buy milk.

Owen was very slim which annoyed everyone because of the volume of food he could eat without putting on any weight. His right arm was covered in a sleeve of tattoos he had spent months agonising over so the inked design would flow exactly as he wanted. Each marking had significance. Owen would often rant about the fickle nature of tattoos and people who followed stupid trends.

"I'm not going to be one of those idiots who gets a Chinese symbol etched into their skin. Ya know, those muppets who think it says *love, peace and harmony* when it actually reads *I'm a dumb English person who likes chicken chow mein.*"

This month he was sporting a beard and ironic moustache that curled up at the ends like that of a circus strongman. He had recently shaved his hair out of frustration and boredom after trying to grow it past his ears, but he thought he looked far too effeminate. So began the giant Moses-style beard that he grew to emphasise his burgeoning masculinity. Owen was an aspiring writer who worked as an editor for a budget travel magazine. This meant nonsensical long hours, last minute assignments but also free trips to some truly dismal hotels in England. He hated his job but so did every bright twenty-five-year-old Londoner with a first-class degree and dreams of being truly awesome one day. You had a crap job because there was little room to be picky when you had extortionate rent to pay, not because selling your soul to Satan looked great on your CV. In Owen's case Satan was his gobshite of a boss who was three years his junior and less experienced.

We all worked out of necessity, not for love. Them be the rules. You must pass go and you must collect £200, just for it to be instantaneously bled from your account by direct debits. His office was in Soho, just around the corner from the bar, which meant he was always a stone's throw away from the high-jinx and debauchery of the London gay scene. Soho was our playground and we probably loved it more than it loved us. The last time we were out, we danced for hours to Kylie's entire back catalogue and then decided to try our hand at busking to raise the cash for a cab home. And by busking I mean shouting every school assembly hymn we could remember into a traffic cone. A random passer-by threw a two-pound coin at me as I began my rendition of "All Things Bright and Beautiful". It wasn't enough for a taxi, but we bought a bag of chips en route to the bus stop. Any excuse to be out drinking in town tonight, even Jason's saddening drinks of death, would get Owen's vote.

The girl at the bar came to pick up our empty glasses from the table. She smiled almost sympathetically at me while Jason continued to listen to his music.

"Same again?" she asked.

"Yes, please, and a pint of cider. My other friend will be here in a bit." As I glanced at the front door, thinking Owen would walk right in on cue. He didn't.

She smiled again. "Will it be a long night for you?"

I tilted my head to the side, slightly confused as to why she would ask that and slightly impressed that she was able to read a situation so well. I sighed deeply and said, "It sure looks that way."

There's something comforting in the smile of a stranger when you really need it the most. It makes you feel bonded for those few moments. You're in it together even though the stranger has no comprehension of the drama unfolding.

The door opening bumped me out of my thoughts, and Owen walked in. He was holding his green backpack in one hand and had already started removing his jacket. Jason spotted him and finally took his earphones out. I guess now he had real guests he had to start acting normal. Owen had a habit of bounding over to you whenever you met, like a giddy puppy expecting treats just for having the waggiest tail. This time, however, his movements were slow and cautious so as not to upset Jason further with his usual gleeful approach. I've never seen his expression so controlled and sombre. With a nod in my direction as he neared our table, he went in for a hug with Jason. Jason squeezed him back and I sat there thinking, *Why the feck didn't I hug him when I arrived?*

"I just ordered you a drink," I said, interrupting the soft manly hug-a-thon before me.

"Ah thanks, my lover. I'm gasping," Owen said, breaking his embrace with Jason and planting a scratchy beardy kiss on my cheek.

The bar girl placed our drinks on the table just as Owen sat down. I motioned to grab my wallet but she stopped me. "You can settle the bill when you leave." And with that she threw another smile my way and sashayed in the direction of the bar. One thing was certain about this exotic bartender: she was the kind of girl who would want to be "just friends" after you'd failed to make her your wife! Pretty girls always wanted to be "just friends."

It was only as Jason struggled to stand that I realised how squiffy he really was. I instinctively threw my body forward anticipating his fall, but he stabilised himself and held his whiskey in the air. I was surprised that only a few drops left the glass.

"Here are the rules," Jason began his public speech.

"Tonight we don't speak of death and all the jive that comes with it. Let's just drink until it's all over."

I didn't dare question what he meant by "all over", because although I knew this morbid emotion well, it now seemed too dark and scary amongst friends. Owen and I raised our glasses and heavy-handedly knocked them together all the same. The pact was made. We were to support Jason by getting inebriated to within an inch of our lives, and I was fine with that.

Chapter Four

Sometimes good old-fashioned alcohol makes for great conversations. If you needed to discuss the politics behind the abolition of the African slave trade or the 1916 Easter Rising and how that had a direct affect on the latest *Eastenders* storyline, then double shots of everything and anything should do it. The subject matter could be completely bonkers, but for that intoxicated period you are convinced you're a freedom fighter who knows everything there is to know about, well, just about everything. Sound reasoning and conversational etiquette are dumped as you scream your opinions into the faces of your friends. Essentially, the loudest person wins. I wasn't long into my sixth double vodka and Coke when I felt the boldness in my speech wrap around me like a warm, fuzzy blanket. I had transformed into a news correspondent with a degree in Middle Eastern politics trying to whip up a mini revolution from my seat in a pub. As I leaned back from my chair to scream "Free Palestine!" to the unsuspecting folks around me, the bar girl broke my flow, interjecting with a polite but intentional cough. "We're closing in fifteen minutes. Would you like to settle the bill?" Shit, it was already 2.30 a.m.

Her accent still perplexed me so instead of answering her, I shouted, "Your accent is fabulous. Where are you from?"

She answered with a smile but not enough to disguise her flushed cheeks. If I had embarrassed her, I didn't care. "I'm from Portugal." She laughed.

Owen smacked his empty glass down onto the table and grinned. "Jolly good! We will pay up and be on our way momentarily! Thank you for your kind hospitality!" he said in a faux-Oxbridge accent.

The bar girl giggled softly but didn't look at me as she said, "*De nada.* You're welcome," and headed back across the room.

All three of us clumsily reached for our wallets, inside jeans pockets and backpacks.

"Right, I'm going to pay! Milkybars are on me kids!" said Jason as he threw what he thought was his credit card on the table.

"I'm pretty sure you can't pay with a Tesco Clubcard mate!" said Owen, smirking at the bravado Jason had tried but failed miserably to lord over us.

"Ah yes. Well that won't do." He reached into his wallet again, laid his Visa down and flicked a good-humoured middle finger at Owen. "I need a piss. Be back in a second," he slurred and scraped the back of his chair across the floor. He stood up with false confidence and zero stability and walked like a toddler towards the toilets. There was no way Jason would be paying tonight. Owen and I would split the bill and worry about being financially ruined when we sobered up. I clumsily reached into my wallet and my work photo ID card fell out. It used to be attached to a bright blue lanyard but I'd lost it months ago. Too impatient to place it back into my wallet I simply stuffed it into the left pocket of my hoodie.

I vigorously rubbed my eyes, signalling the arrival of my bedtime, but I knew the night was far from over. Sometimes I would try to sneak out of pubs once last orders were called and the rest of the guys were drunk enough not to notice. I would have to time it just right; otherwise Owen would catch me edging toward the door and then either use our friendship to guilt me into staying or flatter me with sycophantic comments. Some evenings I just didn't have the stamina to sustain the champagne lifestyle on my can-of-cider budget. Financially and physically this world of alcohol-fuelled shenanigans was breaking me. I would often crave nights in watching trashy reality TV and eating crisps that had missed my mouth and landed on my chest. It wasn't even a guilty pleasure as I felt no guilt in dumbing down and switching off for a few hours.

By the time we'd paid and Jason had made it back from the toilets, we were the only ones left in The Cellar Door. Although the hours had run away from us at a furious speed, the night was still young and nobody was ready to call time or attempt the long and arduous bus journey home. Unfortunately, with it being a Sunday, most bars were closed for the evening, and our options were slim to none. As we exited the bar through the side doors, the night air punched me square in the face, delivering the message that I was indeed off my game. Even though it was after hours, the streets shooting off into Soho were still lit by fuzzy neon lights and hotdog carts that had been condemned by environmental health. The only difference was the muted party vibe one could find on a Saturday night.

"Where are you guys headed?"

I spun around and lost my balance for a moment. It was the bar girl who was now puffing on a rolled-up cigarette, hugging herself with her leather jacket.

"Do you know anywhere we can drink and perhaps have a dance?" Jason piped up next to me.

She inhaled hard on the end of her rollie and replied, "If you're into house parties then I'm heading to a friend's place?"

Was she inviting us to a party? I didn't get it. She's barely spoken before. She gave me nothing but smiles and blushes and now this Portuguese chick was inviting three complete strangers to a house party. But before I could put forward my case of "What the actual fucks!" Owen and Jason had already bounded over to her like two excitable Andrex puppies.

"So I take it we're going, then, lads?" Nobody was listening to me.

"We just have to pick up my friend on the way," the bar girl said, "but the party is only ten minutes' walk from here."

Jason reached out to hold my hand and he swung my arm back and forth as a way of asking for permission to accept Miss Portugal 2006's invitation.

"Okay, okay, as if I have a choice!" I said.

"You always have a choice. I'm Antonia by the way but everyone calls me Toni." She reached out her hand for an awkward and formal handshake.

"I'm Sam. Short for Samantha, but everyone calls me Sam … because, ya know, well, it's shorter."

I had just successfully screwed up a simple introduction. An introduction I should have executed perfectly in GCSE French, never mind English. "Je m'appelle Sam." See – easy! But no, tonight I would stutter and falter the basic of my own mother tongue. Glorious.

"Nice to meet you, Sam!" Toni said.

This time my cheeks flushed, but I'm sure I could've passed it off as the alcohol. Behind Toni's back, just to the right, I could see Owen making a juvenile gesture to suggest cunnilingus. He was mocking me and I retaliated by mouthing "Fuck you" in his direction.

"Where are we headed, then, Toni?" Owen asked.

She flicked the end of her cigarette onto the pavement and turned an intriguing smile on Owen. "We're going to Ulysses!"

Chapter Five

Technically I had to come out to my parents twice. The first time was the biggest anti-climax of my life as I was totally prepared for all manner of disappointment and melodrama. But my father's response was "Oh, okay, dear. Well, that's nice," as he continued to watch the stagnant cricket match on the telly. My mother acknowledged my earth-shattering news from the kitchen: "Well, you've never brought a boy home, so I guess that makes sense."

Bloody ruiners. I was pissed off. Here's me spending years in the closet for fear of being cast out by my middle-class suburban family, and my parents' interest levels peaked at zero point nobody cares. My well-rehearsed coming-out speech ("I'm a person too. This will never change the bond we have") fell on deaf ears. I left the living room crestfallen. This was my moment to be the drama queen – a role I was born to play – and my parents destroyed it with nonchalance. How dare they be more than okay with my sexuality!

The day after the non-event of my coming out, I left suburbia to head back to London, still disgruntled by my parents' lack of interest but with a sense of calm nonetheless. Staring out of the train window, counting the telephone poles speeding past, I thought, *What were the five years of shame for?* I was convinced my parents would disown me for even hinting at the word gay, but they had responded better than I could have ever imagined. I had finally come to terms with that fact that fancying women was not a sin. Despite my love of sci-fi disaster movies, I was never going be punished with fire-and-brimstone vengeance from the heavens. Yet I assumed that God-fearing parents like mine would think my place in hell was now officially confirmed. Come to think of it, setting fire to my brother's school project on volcanoes when I was eight probably fast-tracked my application. But my involvement in a homosexual lifestyle was surely the clincher.

It took me a while to come to terms with the idea of being a gay. I chose to ignore it ever since my head felt light at the first lesbian kiss on the TV soap *Brookside* when I was twelve. How was it possible for two females to kiss so intimately, and why did I have butterflies at the thought of replicating this? I couldn't comprehend why this storyline resonated with me, nor could I shake it from my mind for weeks after the media hype had died down. I wasn't mature enough to understand my new feelings but I sure was mature enough to know that they were wrong and had to be concealed. I simply disregarded my newfound sexual urges as a side effect of puberty!

I revisited these feelings when I was nineteen and one drunken but premeditated kiss outside my university halls of residence led to my first girlfriend. She was hilarious, loud and northern with a wit I had never experienced before. She made me laugh so much that I couldn't help wanting to be close to her. Her confidence and laissez-faire attitude to her sexuality made her that much more attractive. I really envied her this. One evening, watching a VHS tape of *The Bodyguard* under a duvet, she went to hold my hand. Nothing was said as I reciprocated her touch, and we continued to link our fingers in silence until the credits rolled at the end of film.

Two days later, with a little help from Tequila, she finally kissed me. It was sweet and gentle. Her lip-gloss was sticky and tasted of Satsuma, and in that dizzy moment it felt like the most natural thing to do. She was very experienced, so she took the lead. But she always checked my level of comfort and was careful not to frighten me by going too fast. What followed was an intense clandestine relationship. The secrecy was my idea, so of course the relationship was the biggest toxic car crash due to my inability to accept who I was. My out-and-proud girlfriend could only take so much, and once the excitement of a new secret love fizzled out, she made it clear that stepping back into the closet wasn't what she'd signed up for. So she broke up with me two months later and hooked up with a girl much hotter and much gayer than me. The fact that I was head over heels in love with her and that I was enjoying my new sex life didn't give me the courage to hold my girlfriend's hand in public. This simple, innocent act would later take a further two years of practice before it felt normal. It would be two more years before I could openly admit to my friends and myself that I liked kissing women.

I reclined in my seat on the train, blissfully daydreaming of my first lesbian experience, fidgeting and trying to get comfortable. I closed my eyes for a moment and smiled. It was a mini high five to myself. My phone vibrated in my right pocket and despite the No Mobile Phones notices dotted around, I answered, because fuck the police! I was out and proud and lock up your daughters, world, because I was coming to awkwardly woo them.

It was my mother calling and she was crying. Not a quiet whimper but full-on ugly crying. "So when you said you were gay, did you really mean it?" she asked, choking through tears.

My mum had poked a pin in my little bubble of elation and now I had to console her over my preference for vagina over penis. I steadied my voice and said for the second time that weekend, "Yes, I meant it. Mum, I'm gay."

I had to come out to her all over again, and this time I got the full-on dramatics I had originally yearned for. However, as it transpired, I was far from able to handle this queer turn of events.

The next forty-five minutes of my train journey consisted of question after question about whether I will have kids or will I die alone. "Maybe you just need to meet a good Christian boy," she said, obviously thinking that he might pray that pesky gay away. I was astonished that a woman of intelligence like my mother would even utter such outrageous statements. She had told me just a few weeks before that she was thrilled to be invited to a dinner party by her gay work colleague and his partner, and she went into great detail about what a sweet and lovely couple they were. Discovering that her daughter was "one of them" was an entirely different matter, however. Where was the calm, cool and collected parent from yesterday who basically shrugged her shoulders and then continued kneading the bread dough? Who was this hysterical banshee on the other end of the phone asking me the heartbreaking question "What did I do wrong to make you this way?" A lump formed in my throat as I blinked back the tears. I refused to cry in public.

"Mum, I'm going into a tunnel. I'll have to call you back." There was no tunnel but the pressure in my chest was fizzing up and becoming so unbearable that I had to end the call. I craved acknowledgment and I was getting it in spades. Be careful what you wish for. My stupid, stupid heart was stabbing my chest as I doubled over at the shock of what had just happened. The silent high five to myself had been premature. I should have known better. I was an idiot. As the train pulled in to the station, the realisation punched me right in the gut. I feared that being gay was just never going to be okay.

Chapter Six

It was when we cut through another dark alley, with Toni walking ahead of us, that I began to think we were going to be sold as sex slaves to Japanese businessmen. *Surely I'm far too weird looking to be considered sexually attractive*, I thought. Symmetry was not a feature of my face and I was pretty sure my left boob was more rounded than my right. Yes, that is what I would lead with if any advances were made towards me – plead that I'm really ugly and therefore would make a rubbish prostitute. Owen and Jason would indeed be screwed, though. Quite literally. Toni said this place was ten minutes away and we had now been walking for (I tried to focus on my watch) five whole exhausting minutes. I'd give her another five minutes before I huffed and puffed out loud and did absolutely nothing, I decided.

We stopped outside the entrance to a rundown casino where I'm sure all the neon lights of London came to die. A young man was leaning up against the wall outside urinating onto the brickwork and whistling The Black Eyed Peas song "I Gotta Feeling". Disgusting. But without hesitation we all chimed in right on cue when he hit the chorus: "Mazel Tov!"

Still laughing, Owen turned around. "So is this Ulysses?"

Toni smirked and said, "No, no! Firstly, Ulysses is a friend of mine, and secondly, we're just picking up my flat mate Sophie. Her shift should be over now."

As we stood waiting on the street, I noticed Jason was playing with his phone. I walked over and asked him who he was texting.

He looked up sheepishly. "I'm just trying to see if I can get a friend to drop off a little bit of Charlie."

Under normal circumstances I would've vetoed the shit out of this idea, but tonight was not normal. So for the first time my judgement on drugs slipped. I simply rolled my eyes and watched Jason continue to text, squinting at the screen.

Toni lit up another cigarette, and as she blew out a plume of smoke, Owen coughed in an exaggerated manner, fanning the smoke away from his face. He loathed smoking and didn't care that we were standing outside in a public area. He would often tell me how he's far too pretty to die of cancer. Toni didn't take offence at Owen's dramatics and she continued puffing away and playing with the lighter in her other hand.

"Hey, sorry I'm late. My boss is a complete asshole and made me take a last minute stock take of the bar. So I did what any decent law-abiding employee would do."

A slim girl with swept-back hair dressed in an all-black uniform opened one side of her coat to reveal a large bottle of vodka. "Sssh! Don't tell anyone!" She came skipping out of the casino's doorway, and gave Toni a high five.

"This is Sophie. Sophie, these are my new friends who refused to leave my bar, so I brought them with me!"

Owen and I waved, but Jason went right in for an embrace.

"Down boy!" Owen said as Sophie stepped back from this random guy trying to hug her. Jason was far too keen most of the time, without the encouragement of alcohol, but in his defence, nobody was aware at that point that Sophie didn't do hugs.

There was no denying that on first impressions Sophie was quite beautiful. I was of the opinion that beauty was somewhat distorted. It intimidated the likes of me who struggled with the concept. My unease around the bold and the beautiful was based on assumption, and previous experience suggested that pretty girls relied too much on their looks and would cut you in half with bitchy comments. But something about Sophie and her casual response when Toni said she had smudged her eyeliner made me think that she was a good egg. Sophie untied her brown hair and shook it like one of those unattainable airbrushed models in a shampoo advert. Then she furiously stuffed her flat pumps into her bag and exchanged them for eye-watering heels. Sophie must've noticed me gasping as she put on her fancy shoes while leaning on Toni for balance.

"My motto in life is go high or go home!" She reached out her hand and said "Hi, I'm Sophie!"

This time I was determined to get it right. "I'm Sam. Nice to meet you!"

There were no nerves or blushing or stammering. I was getting better at this introduction thing.

"I take it we're off to Ulysses?" Sophie said as she straightened up, now two foot taller, and applied lip-gloss.

"You know it, *bebé!*" Toni replied, and with that she linked arms with Sophie and led us away from the light pollution of the casino.

"It's five minutes this way, I promise you guys!" Toni turned around and smiled directly at me as if she knew I would be the only person who'd feel the need to moan. I blushed again. What was wrong with my cheeks! It must be the alcohol, I told myself.

"Do we need to pick up some booze?" Owen asked as we headed down Old Compton Street.

Sophie turned and called over her shoulder, "You'll have all you need when we get there. I just 'borrowed' this bottle of vodka because I hate my boss!"

I didn't know if it was the glare of the streetlights or my inability to be sober, but Sophie seemed to have two different coloured eyes. I was clearly far more pissed than I had thought.

For the first time that evening I remembered my boss and the fact that I had a job I was supposed to be at in five and a half hours. But I hadn't factored that into my night even before Jason had called, so there was no use pretending I cared now. "What time do you have to work tomorrow?" I called out to Owen, who was walking right next to me.

"I have to be in Brighton by midday tomorrow to check out this hotel for another sodding review. But it's fine. I'll just get the train down later."

Owen was a lot more hardcore than me. I think he had a little Irish in his family, so his stamina for drinking and having the craic was impressive. He could be out all night and roll into work the next day fresh as a daisy and sometimes still high, but he had some insane superpower that enabled him to function without getting fired. Jason I assumed had no intention to work. I didn't want to ask him seeing as it could lead to discussion of the subject that had brought us together tonight.

We finally walked into Soho Square, which was a familiar spot for all of us. When there were those rare days of sunshine in the city that tricked us all into thinking we lived in the Mediterranean, Soho Square was the place to be. The boys and I had spent long summer days lying on the grass quaffing cans of cider and cheap no-name Russian vodka that tormented our livers. It was one of my favourite places in the city and was ideal for people-watching and judging everyone who walked past. But in the early hours of a late-September morning, it was just too cold and miserable to feel any warmth towards the square. I looked around and thought, *What the hell am I doing here?* We continued to walk for another fifty metres until Toni stopped outside of a grand Georgian building that looked like any other converted office building in the West End. "We're here!"

Owen, Jason and I all looked at each other. *THIS is Ulysses' gaff?* I thought. Sophie pressed the third buzzer down on the intercom beside the imposing front door and waited for a reply. There was nothing but static at first, and then we heard loud, distorted dance music. I leaned further into the archway of the door, interested in what would happen next. A squealing, camp voice broke through the din. "Heeeeey guuuurls! Come on up!"

With a click the door automatically unlatched itself and Sophie pushed it open with a giggle. "Welcome to Ulysses!"

Chapter Seven

We climbed two sets of industrial metal stairs until we came to a
small dark landing with a single bulb hanging from the ceiling.
Toni took the lead as we all huddled behind each other. She
rapped the door with her knuckles just as Jason, who was
lagging behind, came running into us. Behind the door you could
just make out a heavy bass line and general chatter. I looked
down at my watch and pinched the side button to illuminate the
digital face. It was 3:20 a.m. The door finally swung open and
what can only be described as an Asian version of Liberace
stood before us. He was wearing a bright yellow vest with the
tightest white trousers, wide-rimmed red sunglasses and was
dripping in enough sparkle to make Elizabeth Taylor's collection
look poor. He looked us up and down and screamed,
"Daaaaarlings!" From here on in the air kisses came thick and
fast as we were ushered inside.

   "Ulysses sweetheart, I would like you to meet my new
friends!" As Toni quickly introduced us all while we shed our
coats and hoodies, which were scooped up and thrown into a
room off the hallway. Ulysses beckoned us through the hall
towards the bass line and the chatter I had heard from outside.
His place was insane, drenched in a thick layer of decadence.
We had just entered what can only be described as a warehouse-
style apartment triple the size of the modest two-bedroom flat

Owen and I shared. A huge purple chandelier hung loudly from the ceiling and the furniture was ironically mismatched in a stylish and intentional way. There was nothing generic about this place. I clocked the gold-leaf mirror on the wall next to the jukebox and the giant pinball machine. I took my phone out of my front pocket and played with it between my fingers.

"Drinks?" Sophie handed us all an unknown liquid tinged a shade of pink.

"It's one of my secret recipes," Ulysses chimed, encouraging us to sample his cocktail so we could critique it straight away. I gulped it down out of sheer confusion. It tasted like strawberry Bon Bons and a shit load of rum. It smarted my eyes and I coughed at the alcohol warming my chest. I hated rum but I was sobering up and I needed to get back on it. I closed my eyes, took another sip and gave Ulysses the thumbs up.

The room was buzzing with at least thirty other people who looked to be in their mid to late twenties. Everyone looked stunning, as if we had just walked into a photo shoot for *Britain's Next Top Model*. Some were draped over each other like they were at a sinful Ancient Greek symposium and others were engaged in deep conversation. Jason was holding two glasses in his hand and talking directly into Sophie's ear in the kitchen. Owen was sitting down on a patchwork armchair signalling for help across the room. It looked like Ulysses' crotch was almost resting on his shoulder. I laughed and waved. I would go and save him in a minute, right after I had sourced another drink.

I sauntered over to the far side of the room with a false sense of purpose. I wanted those around me to be aware that I had intended to come in my damp T-shirt and battered trainers. I cringed. I'd never felt so out of place in my life. I found Toni by the bar area which was in fact an ornate table covered in a smorgasbord of every possible spirit and vintage champagne that I couldn't pronounce and would never be able to afford.

"So, what made you trust three complete strangers enough to bring us to a fabulous house party?" I asked the back of Toni's head. She smelt amazing like sweet exotic potions in an apothecary store. I was being weird. I needed to stop sniffing the back of her head, so I backed up slowly as she turned around.

"I could see your friend was having a sad evening and needed cheering up. And you were really patient with me when I messed up your drinks order." It was my turn to smile. "Plus I think you needed a distraction."

I poured a sizeable measure of vodka into my glass and said, "It's my friend Jason who needs the distraction. He's had a truly terrible day."

But it was as if Toni had decided to disregard this. "No Sam, I think it is you who needed this more than him. Something in your expression when you approached the bar seemed like it was, how do you say, broken?"

She picked up the mini umbrella that sat at the side of her glass, sucked the end of the cocktail stick and placed it behind my ear. I think I preferred Toni when she was just smiley and mute. She was talking in riddles and she was far too new for me to tell her to shut up and get out of my head.

"So how do you know Ulysses?" I needed to fill the awkward silence with a change of subject.

"He's mine and Sophie's landlord. We have a flat in London Bridge. Nothing like this! He always invites us to his parties, and so here we are!"

I didn't know what I had been expecting but it wasn't that. In my mind Ulysses was their pimp or some eccentric uncle who just so happens to throw these grandiose shindigs. But a landlord? That sounded far too pedestrian.

"You must check out his roof terrace. You can see all the way to Canary Wharf from there!"

I'm pretty sure you couldn't but Toni's excitement intrigued me and I wanted to be on the same fun bus as her.

"Go save your friend. Uly will eat him alive!" Toni said.

Shit. I had forgot about Owen.

"There are steps going to the roof at the side of the kitchen. I'll meet you up there." And with that she strutted towards the kitchen area where Jason was no doubt trying his best to crack on to Sophie.

The way in which a person walked speaks volumes about their character. The engineering of an individual's walk opens a little window into their soul. There is of course the obvious shoulders-back, head-up, calculated saunter that masks certain insecurities. Then there's the bouncing swagger of a walk that suggests a cocksure attitude. And sometimes, when people-watching in

Soho Square, I would notice at least one person with drooped shoulders and slow, steady paces who avoided eye contact as they walked. These folks look so downcast. It was as if it physically pained them to put one foot in front of the other. I would want to run over and give them a free hug or a simple high five just so they'd know that despite their best attempt of hiding, I had noticed them. I sometimes wished somebody would notice me. As Toni walked away from me, she looked very confident, and her hips swayed as if she were traversing the runway at London Fashion Week. The eyes of Ulysses' guests turned to watch her or, more than likely, the curvature of her arse.

Pushing the image of Toni's arse to the back of my mind, I hurled myself onto Owen's lap and kissed his hairy cheek. I didn't know how to break up this uncomfortable moment between him and our host, so I figured throwing myself into the middle would help.

"Ulysses, your place is fab!" I exclaimed after shattering the sexual tension.

"Oh honey, please call me Uly. I got this place in the court settlement with my heinous ex-partner, who ran off with some twinky Argentinean boy after thirteen years!"

I wasn't even nearly prepped enough for this conversation and I had noticed that Sophie, Toni and Jason had already left the kitchen and must be up on the roof.

"Oh wow! That sounds like a crazy story! I'm going to need another drink!" I boldly extended my newly empty glass.

Uly laughed and said, "I'll be right back, sweetheart!" He headed off to fill my glass with more toxic liquid. As soon as his back was turned, I grabbed Owen's arm and whispered playfully, "Come with me if you want to live!"

Chapter Eight

Working in customer service wasn't exactly my dream job. Mainly because I found it hard to disguise my disinterest in whether or not your refuse bin was emptied on time. My voice would say, "How can I bend over backwards and help you in this plight?" but there was always a go-fuck-yourself tone to my "Have a nice day!" The fact that I arrived for the interview hungover from a music festival the day before, showed just how committed I was to the job. I needed to pay my rent, and the recruitment agency had pitched the position to me as "a casual, young environmental company". I liked casual and young and all things Captain Planet. It was in reality a call centre for a bin company, where the entire staff was made up of students who were only there to save enough cash to go travelling. I was the sole twenty-something graduate who had no end game. The mortification set in quickly.

All I had was a degree in a subject that would prevent me from ever earning enough to live a comfortable lifestyle. BA Hons Media Studies should have been renamed *BA ha ha! Just joking! You'll be working at a Blockbuster video store for the rest of your life.* So when my colleagues, who were brimming with ambition and had an average age of a fertilised embryo, asked me what I had planned for the future, I lied. Depending on the day of the week I was either saving up to travel the world or to fund my tuition fees for a masters in biomechanical engineering. No matter what, nobody could know how much my life lacked direction and how I was getting closer and closer to moving back in with the parents. Anything was better than answering the phones within three rings to irate supermarkets calling to demand why their recycling bin hadn't been collected that morning. Even the noose of suburbia.

When I finished my degree I actually wanted to teach. I figured that I could inspire kids to be confident and proud human beings, something that my schoolteachers failed to accomplish with me. Despite all the detentions I clocked up and all the trips to the headmaster's office for being a lively, insubordinate child, I still wanted to set an example. I wanted to prove that I was capable of being responsible, of encouraging individuals to be true to themselves and still play by the rules, while at the same time avoiding the asphyxiating chains of conformity. But I was stuck between wanting to make a difference and bone-idle laziness. The only effort I made to research my route into teaching was picking up a handful of leaflets at a careers fair. These were quickly lost among final-demand bills.

I had drive, certainly, but it fluctuated and manifested itself at odd times of the day such as during bus journeys, while ordering a coffee from the jolly Hungarian man at the train station or when I wanted to sleep. It was during these moments that I wanted to save the world, make a difference and stand up and be counted. I wanted to be someone my parents were proud of and not another "she had potential but what a shame she never applied herself" person. I had so much enthusiasm for bettering my position in life, but by the time my bus journey had ended, my coffee cup was empty and I had drifted off to sleep, the self-doubt had settled back in and the procrastination began all over again. It appeared that I was nixing my own ambitions with sheer laziness.

It was my father who would always remind me that I could be anything I wanted to be. He loved a good old rant thinly veiled as a pep talk. Every time I visited home, he enquired as to whether I was still a bin lady. I would retaliate with "I'm not a bin lady, but there's nothing wrong with that profession, Dad." Even though I didn't physically empty bins, I did orchestrate it, so he wasn't far wrong.

"Well, when people ask me what you do, I say you work in IT," my dad would say.

Working in IT was apparently a far more respectable career choice than having to admit to his friends that I had failed to reach my potential in life. My father knew I hated my job and when I was home he would often hijack my precious television viewing time just when my favourite soap was on. "So what is it that you really want from life Samantha? Because I didn't work two jobs for all those years putting you and your brother through good schools and university just so you could piss your education up the wall by emptying bins!" I would lower myself further and further into the sofa hoping the cushions would envelope my entire body. I wanted to slip down the sides where all the two-pence pieces, missing buttons and crumbs from last week's dinner were hiding.

The one-sided conversation would usually end with me rolling my eyes and acting like a bratty child as he banged on and on about how I need to "grab life by the balls and swing on them". Although I would squirm, it was only because I knew he was right. I wasn't fulfilling my dreams and I lacked the passion to do anything about it. I knew that, he knew that, but I just couldn't bring myself to admit it out loud. I was wasting the best years of my life by inviting obstacles into my world. I wasn't enjoying myself and the worst thing about it was, I was allowing it.

The only aspect of my daily grind that kept me going most days was the knowledge that my friends were also in equally loathsome jobs. We all went to university and graduated with worthy enough grades to put on a CV, but for some reason the opportunity to explore our true passion never arose. There was that sad but reassuring truth, and also my little pal Kai on the end of the phone. He worked at the head office of the bin company and if shit went down, which happened every other hour for me, he was the bloke to talk to. We instantly hit it off with our love of inappropriate humour. You certainly know you have a friend for life if you willingly laugh at taboo subjects, admit that you would probably be locked up if your phone lines were tapped but continue to laugh in the face of danger all the same. He was the male version of me – crude and rude – and he kept me sane. We always promised each other that we would meet for a drink but after saying this for a year and a half. I think we were both fully aware that it would be like a creepy blind date and neither of us wanted to shatter the illusion. So phone buddies we would remain.

Maybe my sadistic English literature teacher was right. Maybe I wouldn't amount to anything and the thought of making a dent in the world was as ridiculous as the time said teacher erupted into fits of evil laughter when I said I wanted to pursue my love of the English language. I had hopes and dreams but the monotony of the real world was draining all my determination to prove my doubters wrong. I figured that there might always be the haunting sensation that you are wasting your life no matter what path you took, but I felt like I was living this fear in real time. When do you get to the point where you throw your arms up in the air and shout, "Enough is enough"? The once-solid and legitimate reasons for staying in London were becoming shaky. Any real enthusiasm I once had for the big smoke became clouded with every, "Hello, you're through to Sam. How can I help you today?"

Chapter Nine

Although I was wearing my beer jacket, I was thankful Uly didn't scrimp on the outdoor décor, as the roof terrace was home to two huge patio heaters. My bare arms surely would have died of hypothermia otherwise. Just my arms, as that's obviously how science works. As Owen and I climbed to the roof, we could see the rest of the guys leaning, laughing and pointing over the balcony. Toni may have been exaggerating the extent of the view, but it really was vast and spectacular. The sheer magnitude of the city lay ahead, the lights like fireflies, and we five drunkards were nothing more than a speck.

"So you managed to escape the clutches of Uly?" Sophie joked with Owen.

"He was just about to launch into his story about his ex leaving him for an Argentinean boy!" Owen said, feigning disbelief, just as Toni handed us each a flute of champagne.

Both girls laughed knowingly, clearly well aware of the story.

"Lets make a roast!" Jason declared, talking from one side of his mouth so that his cigarette would remain between his lips.

"You mean a *toast*, right?" I said as he rolled his eyes and removed the cigarette.

"To making each day count!" Owen raised his glass, a glint in his eye.

"No," said Jason, "that sounds like some bullshit from a greeting card! Here's to new friends, fun times and drinking until we puke!"

Jason was one fist pump and a penis tug away from being a jock. But we all cheered like football hooligans and chinked our glasses together like the cast of a cheesy American sitcom.

After a few more toasts to ridiculous hopes and aspirations such as Jason's wish to sustain an erection when he's romancing ladies in his eighties, we all made ourselves comfortable on the giant floor cushions. There was a small wooden coffee table and tea lights in mason jars scattered around us. I bet Uly had lured many a young plaything up there. Toni reached over me to grab the second bottle of champagne, and as her black jumper fell up her arm, I noticed the tattoo on the inside of her wrist. It was written in a language I didn't recognise and surrounded by some sort of stencilled flower arrangement. I was about to ask her about it when Jason produced a clear packet of white powder from his jeans pocket that must have been there all this time. "So, who wants to get a little buzzy with me?"

I like to keep an open mind, and in the grand scheme of things people could do as they pleased. We all make our choices and I had always believed that the responsibility lies with the individual. Unless their choice has a direct effect on your life or well-being, everyone should just take a breath, calm down and mind your own damn business. However everyone is also entitled to an opinion and for many years leading up to that moment on Uly's roof terrace, I was a strong advocate of the

Just Say No drugs campaign. I had witnessed the effect of drugs on my friends before and it had never appealed to me. I could reach a euphoric plane on sweet liquor alone without tripping out talking to fairies and chasing mythical dragons into my back garden. Alcohol was my drug of choice and that was all I could handle. My mind was a murky place at best, and unleashing my subconscious onto the world through a little rabbit hole of class-A madness could spell my downfall, I felt.

"Absolutely not!" Sophie screeched in response to Jason waving his little bag of corruption around. "Do what you want, Jason, but I am judging you so hard right now." It was safe to say that this girl was not a fan of naughty overindulgence and neither was she afraid to say exactly what she thought. "Poppycock! I will not be privy to this absolute nonsense." Her vocabulary veered towards the ridiculous the more champagne she sank. I wanted to applaud her for shoehorning *poppycock* into a sentence but I figured that it wasn't the time.

Sophie's conviction would have had more an impact if she hadn't stumbled when she got up to leave. Maybe it was the heels she couldn't walk in, or maybe it was the fact that she was as wasted as the rest of us. Either way I could see right down her low-cut top as she tried to regain her balance, and my brain suddenly turned into that of a teenage boy.

"I'm not really up for that tonight. I have work tomorrow, so I'll go with her," Owen said. He jumped up with as much enthusiasm as the evening's binge drinking would allow and followed Sophie down the stairs.

"Is she always like that?" Jason asked. "Ya know, sensible and really, really loud?"

Toni laughed out loud and answered, "She just likes to play by the rules. There are no grey areas with Sophie. But she sticks to her guns and that's what I love about her. Sometimes she is all the way crazy and outrageous and other times she just wants to lie on the couch, drink tea and watch TV. I blame her split personality on her eyes!"

"Her what?" I said.

"She has heterochromia – two different-coloured eyes. So depending on her mood, I usually say it's the influence of her brown eye or blue eye!"

I hadn't made it up then.

I still hadn't decided if I was going to follow Owen and Sophie down to the party, but for the moment I made no attempt to remove myself from the situation. Jason had already cut three lines of the powder with his Tesco Clubcard and was now rolling a twenty-pound note. Toni and I looked on silently and continued to drink.

I had never snorted anything up my nose before and the thought of it sounded disgusting. The noise coming from Jason and Toni sounded so guttural and uncouth, but I still sat there spellbound. I could've left at any time but the intrigue and odd sense of wonderment was too enticing. Toni handed me the rolled up note so I guessed it was my turn.

"Just place one finger over the other nostril and inhale it all in one go," Jason told me. "Don't stop and don't blow it out, because this shit cost me eighty quid!"

No pressure then. As I hovered over the table my heart pounded an irregular beat. I panicked and hurriedly sucked it all up. It felt like it had hit the back of my brain and I coughed. I could then feel it sliding down my throat. It tasted bitter and dry and I coughed again. Jason smacked me on the back in a congratulatory fashion and laughed at me. "See, nothing to it!" He cut more of the powder. "Tuck in ladies! I need another piss! Excuse me for a moment." Jason ran to the stairs and disappeared downwards.

I lay back on the cushion and stared up at the inky sky. I had just had my first line of cocaine. I didn't feel anything at all so I pulled out my phone. I noticed I only had 32 per cent battery left and that it was now 4.40 a.m. As I closed the flip phone, I noticed Toni looming over me. She moved a strand of her long dark hair behind her ear and inched towards me. I didn't move. In fact I didn't dare move for fear that I was already high and imagining this moment. She leaned in and planted a kiss on my lips. Her nose was freezing when it touched mine, but her lips were full, warm and moist.

"Why did you do that?" I whispered.

"Because I wanted to." She gently took the forgotten cocktail umbrella from behind my ear and leaned in again, but this time she slowly ran her tongue across my lips. With a cheeky smile she then rolled back over to her own giant cushion next to me.

My brain didn't have time to process whatever had just happened, but I knew that I wanted more. The unexpected interlude came to an end as Jason burst back onto the terrace, fixing the zip on his flies. I bolted upright and adjusted myself into a seated position. I wanted another line.

Chapter Ten

Jason hadn't changed much since school. He was still very good-looking in a blonde, blue-eyed, boy-band way. The girls would ogle him on the football field as I sat bored and rolling my eyes to the point of fatigue. He was always immaculately groomed, smelling of the latest designer aftershave and embracing fashion fads no matter how stupid he looked or how form-fitting his trousers were. Jason oozed the kind of confidence that made you trust him even when he was clueless. I'm sure that was how he landed his job in marketing and was promoted within a month to head of his team and given a company car. The gift of the gab, some would say. I would say he was an eloquent bullshitter! With his designer stubble and a waistline that was slightly bigger these days, to accommodate his diet of beers and kebabs, Jason was still as animated as his seventeen-year-old self.

I initially didn't like him. He had dumped one of my friends and left her heartbroken. Well, as much heartbreak as one could expect from sixteen-year-olds who had dated for two whole weeks. So, based on nothing but my friend's word, I had already decided that Jason was bad news. I headed up my one-woman hate campaign against him. I would walk past him in the school corridors and mumble "Wanker!" just loud enough so he would hear. I continued to do this for three consecutive days, and on the fourth day he turned around and asked me directly what my problem was and why I hated him so much. I was stunned that he was calling me out on my attitude and I had no smart comeback. Instead I apologised meekly and protested that I didn't actually hate him; I was just supporting my friend and her bruised ego. From that day onwards I always said hello to him and the hellos eventually turned into conversation, and the conversations revealed common interests and a shared outlandish sense of humour.

Lying on Uly's roof terrace, I felt completely sober for the first time in hours, but I couldn't stop talking. My speech was stretched and filled with lusty tones. Every word that left my mouth was punctuated with passion and sensuality. The erratic rhythm of the night had fallen away to leave a sweet rock-steady beat. I felt like we were on Jamaica time. Toni was now lying across my lap and playfully flirting, making slow ticklish circles on my palms with her fingers. We had just finished a conversation on how we were all going to open a new bar in Soho with a casino in the back for Sophie to host and possibly steal things from, when I realised I really needed the toilet. I glanced down at Toni who was now puffing perfect smoke circles into the air. Why did she tease me with that kiss? And would we ever talk of it again? I leant into her and whispered, "I'll be back in a moment. Nature calls."

"Don't be long," she cooed back at me, seducing me all over again with that smile.

My body felt like a dead weight as I scrambled over to the stairs. I pushed the doors into the main living room where the mood had changed from exotic rave to peaceful Indian ashram. There were bodies lying on the floor and draped over chairs, and the jukebox was now playing what sounded like a sitar version of every Adele song ever written. I looked down at my watch; it read 5.12 a.m. Where were Sophie and Owen? Where was Uly? And where was the blasted toilet?!

I opened one door off of the hallway, where our coats were housed. It was dark and I could make out a few moans and what seemed like six different bodies moving rhythmically next to the window. This was definitely not the toilet, unless the toilet was a sex den. I hastily left and knocked on the door opposite trying to push the handle down. The door was locked, and with my bladder close to exploding, I let out a "For fuck's sake!" There was a muffled noise inside and then "Sam, is that you?" The door unlocked and I had reached the promise land! "Friends!" I shouted with much relief and comfort.

Uly was passed out in an empty vintage bathtub, with a saffron coloured silk scarf around his neck. Sophie was sitting on the toilet with the lid closed, sporting a huge, Indian, feathered headdress, and Owen was on the carpeted floor propped up against the side of the tub. "Have you finished being a disgusting junkie?" Sophie spat with an accusatory tone. I laughed because I couldn't take her attitude seriously while she was dressed like one of the Village People. I went to hug her but her body language suggested she would blind me with mace spray if I did.

"I really need a wee, or I'm quite happy to piss on the floor at this stage." I said.

Sophie reluctantly removed herself from the toilet seat and motioned me to use it.

"Are you both staying for this?" I was now shifting my weight between both legs sure that the search for a toilet was pointless seeing as I was now going to urinate onto Uly's shag carpet.

"I would move if I could but I can't. I promise I won't look." Owen then covered his eyes with his hands as if that gesture shielded him from my act of peeing.

"And I have a vagina too, so I have no interest in watching you wee." I really couldn't cope with Sophie's attitude right now but her semi-aggression oddly made me like her a lot. With a reluctant sigh, I pulled down my jeans, then underwear and sat on the porcelain pot.

It was only when I began washing my hands in front of the mirror that I noticed how eerie my eyeballs looked. I removed my watch, placed it on the edge of the hand basin and threw cold water onto my face. Opening my eyes, I realised that this simple movement was a re-enactment. My day was repeating itself.

I was feeling really light, a kind of excited sense of invincibility, and I was ready to tell the guys about Toni kissing me until Owen jumped in.

"Sam, I've done something dreadful?" He was slurring his words.

I shook my hands dry and then wiped them on the back of my jeans.

"What?" I replied, annoyed.

Sophie sat back on the toilet and began giggling.

"Do you want the good news or the bad news?" Owen continued in a tone that made me think that the good news would be equally as distressing as the bad news.

"The bad news …"

Owen lowered his head and whispered, "I allowed Uly to kiss me and, and, and … I may have touched him in a non-PG manner."

Sophie's giggles became louder. Owen had just rendered my news with Toni null and void.

"You're gross and you're going to a sex clinic as soon as we get home!" Owen's promiscuity was one thing I couldn't abide. I mean if you're going to have sexual relations with someone at least make sure they're not your dad's age and didn't look like an amalgamation of every Gay Pride float since 1972.

"Is this why he's unconscious in the bath? You lulled him to sleep with fellatio?"

Owen straightened up and said matter-of-factly, "He told me I had nice eyes and gave me another drink! You know I'm weak when strangers compliment me and give me treats!"

I tried to conceal my smile. "And the good news?"

Sophie rubbed her hands together like a scheming Scooby Doo villain, "This is the good bit!" she squealed.

Owen reached into his back pocket, produced a set of keys and jingled them at me. "Uly lent me his car so I don't have to get the train to Brighton later. We're going on a road trip, Sam!"

Chapter Eleven

"Absolutely not!"

"But, Sam, why?" Owen whined like a child who'd missed out on his nap that afternoon.

"Because, Owen, we live in a democratic society and because I enjoy forced fun and taking a vote on silly suggestions!" It was true, I did. "And none of us are in any condition to operate heavy machinery. Let me just go get Jason and Toni and then we can all decide on this potentially suicidal road trip." As I turned into the hallway I could hear Owen's failed attempt at a whisper: "She's such a fucking ruiner."

Invigorated by a mischievous sense of fun and equally wanting to spill the beans about Owen's indiscretion, I bounded up the steps to the roof terrace. The night sky had become much lighter signalling sunrise was around the corner. I walked across the terrace just as Jason was adjusting the crotch area of his jeans. He met my face with an odd expression and Toni shot up off the cushions. Her jumper was discarded to one side and one of her trouser legs was carelessly rolled up.

"Urmm, hi!" I said.

Toni's cheeks were flushed but I was sure that wasn't my doing this time. "Were you guys doing what I think you were doing?" I didn't know how to play things down or act aloof. I wanted and needed to know what the hell I had just missed.

"Yeah. We finished the cocaine. I apologise but you took too long!" Jason was a master of distraction and usually I would call him out on it, but I was aware of his lack of clarity right now. Plus Toni's face said it all.

"We're going on a road trip," I barked. Democracy was dead. A totalitarian regime was required and I would be calling the shots now. Me and my bruised ego wanted to get as far away as possible from this hotbed of sexual depravity, and I was going with or without them.

"But you can't drive?" Jason said as if logic was now his new thing. "Owen will drive. Uly's given him the keys." I said trying to keep my irritation in check. Jason's face lit up at the news of something else to add to the list of crazies that had occurred so far. Toni, whose name I would have happily substituted with slut right now, still refused to make eye contact with me.

I always seemed to get myself caught up in these ill-timed expressions of lust, mostly as a crash test dummy for straight girls. It's like I was a gigantic lezzy punch bag for heterosexual women and their pent-up sexual frustration. A friend at work once cornered me in the toilets on a staff night out and told me how she couldn't stop thinking about me and how she wondered what it would be like to kiss me. Bewildered, I was powerless as she proceeded to stab the back of my throat with her tongue. And then, just to prove how much she wanted to explore her sexuality with me, she shagged Nigel in accounts that very same night. I had never felt so attractive in my whole life. Another straight pal accosted me as we walked to the night bus in

Trafalgar Square one evening. After she felt me up by the base of Nelson's column, she avoided me for two weeks. She finally called me and asked if she could be my girlfriend. I did us both a favour and blocked her number. I have since lived my life vicariously through episodes of *The L Word*.

I had only fallen in love once and I vowed never to do it again. I was fifteen and she was my best friend. Her heterosexuality filtered from every part of her personality, style and attitude but I was far too blinded by her warmth towards me. I had never had a close friend who was a girl, so I confused these feelings of newness with something else. She was popular and attractive in an effortless way, which had all the boys at school lining up for dates with her. She would play it down and act blasé, which only made the lads like her more. She always sat next to me at lunch and woodwork classes, amusing me with funny stories and over-the-top impressions of Mrs Price, our PE teacher who we all not so secretly hated. She made me feel shy and naked when she was around me, muting my voice. She stripped back a layer of my personality that had never been exposed before. Even when the boys approached her with overpowering aftershave and floppy hair preened with Brylcreem, she ignored them until we had finished our latest Mrs Price rant. She, made my stomach spasm.

One day, whispering and giggling behind the bookshelves in the library, I could no longer hide my feelings for her. I had a piece of fluff in my hair and she motioned her hand to remove it. The palm of her hand brushed against the side of my cheek and it sent a gazillion volts through my body. As she continued explaining how her history homework was ruining her life, I followed the movements of her mouth, mesmerised and wondering what she tasted like. Without engaging my brain I leant in and softly kissed her lips. She stumbled backwards and the look on her face broke my heart a thousand times over. She roughly wiped her lips with the back of her hand, with an enraged look of disgust on her face.

"What the hell are you playing at, Sam?" She shrieked, loud enough for the entire library to hear.

I tried to form words but I remained silent. How had I got this so wrong?

That night after school, I cried so hard I thought my chest would collapse in on itself. My mother heard me sobbing and came into my room and sat on the edge of my bed, patiently waiting for an explanation. I didn't want to talk about it, and how would I explain kissing a girl anyway? My mum flung her arms around me and cradled me. She never asked me what was wrong, and simply being held until the tears stopped was all I really needed from her.

My now ex-best friend avoided me like the plague, so we silently agreed to ignore each other at school. She had a new group of friends who were like a cackling pack of witches stirring a cauldron of gossip and bitchy remarks, and I began hanging around with the boys again. I would sometimes notice her looking at me in class but I was too nervous and humiliated to return her gaze. I prayed for the summer holidays to arrive so

I could sellotape my busted heart back together before term started again.

The sound of footsteps climbing to the roof brought me back to the present. Toni looked up and all three of us turned to face the noise. Sophie, breathless and unstable on her feet, came hurtling towards us. It was only as she drew closer that I could see the panic on her face. "It's … it's Uly," she spluttered. "He won't wake up!"

Chapter Twelve

The first time I saw Owen cry we were watching *Brokeback Mountain*. It was after an evil hangover, inflicted by a night of drinking a bottle of Patrón he'd picked up at a Spanish airport. I'd hated tequila ever since my twentieth birthday party, when I'd downed a shot, immediately threw up into my hand and then wiped it on the barstool next to me. But it was free booze and only idiots passed on free booze. We closed all the curtains in the living room to intensify our melancholy self-pity and watched the movie. As the last scene faded to darkness, we both wanted to denounce our homosexuality. I saw Owen rub his eyes and I jabbed him in the ribs for being such a baby. We later had to watch a few episodes of *Will and Grace* to drag us out of the slump we were in.

The second time I saw Owen cry was as he furiously tried to wake Uly by throwing handfuls of water onto his face. Uly's lips were dry and pale grey.

The first time I saw a dead body was when my auntie died. I was eleven and I remember trying to leave the church at the end of the service so I didn't have to walk past her open coffin. I was following my brother through the back door, but there were so many people I lost him in the crowd. A sea of black faces came towards me and I was swept up into the bodies going in the opposite direction. As I battled on, determined to not follow the procession to the coffin, an old black lady with her hair in a tight grey bun glared down at me with flared nostrils. "Where do you think you're going? You have to pay your respects." I was petrified and couldn't form the words to tell her how much I detested the idea of seeing my dead aunt. Defeated and whipped into obedience, I lowered my head, turned around and slowly walked with the masses to the front of the church. I planned to close my eyes once I got there so I didn't have to see anything, but then as I approached the mahogany box my head emptied. I only peeked down for a moment but it was a moment that stole many nights' sleep from me.

My aunt didn't look peaceful. The expression on her charcoal face seemed furious. Maybe she didn't like the blue organza dress she was made to wear or the white gloves that did nothing for her complexion. Her head was wrapped in an ivory silk scarf similar in style to the head wraps she'd worn in her final months as the chemotherapy ravaged her. Similar in style, but lacking in the vibrant peacock colours I was accustomed to seeing her in. She was such a loud and lively lady and my heart ached to see her confined in a wooden box, dressed in an outfit I knew she would have hated. Her disappointed cold face would be etched in my mind for many years to come.

"Who was with him last?" Toni shouted.

"Well … we were." Sophie said, a tearful whimper to her voice.

Toni pushed Owen out of the way and jumped into the bath. She tried to find a pulse and then began frantically slapping Uly.

"Come on, you crazy old fool. Wake up! Don't be silly. You have to get up!" Upon the fourth slap Uly's head fell to the side and his eyelids parted, but his eyes were rolled back in his head. He looked like something out of a horror movie and the shock propelled Toni backwards.

"He's dead, isn't he?" Owen stammered.

"Yes he is." Jason joined the conversation from the doorway. "And we're all very much fucked."

I couldn't think over Sophie's sobbing let alone articulate a sentence. I hadn't seen a dead body for twelve years. I didn't even look when Kai at work sent me an email attachment of some gangster rapper's dead corpse a few months back. I didn't fancy the nightmares. Yet now a real-life nightmare lay before me and there was no opportunity to click Delete on my keyboard and expunge the image from my eyes.

"Sam, do you think I killed him? Maybe I gave him a heart attack?" Owen said.

"Owen, please just shut the hell up and let me think!" I was rubbing the back of my neck but still all intelligent thought was out of reach.

"He was alive when he got into the bath and he told us he just wanted to take a nap." Sophie lamented.

"We need to get out of here." Jason spoke frankly, with no emotion.

Of all of us stood staring into the bathtub, Jason was the last one I expected to talk with sense. His suggestion was met with a barrage of "you insensitive bastard" insults from the rest of the group.

"He's right. We can't stay here. The flat is covered with random people, alcohol and drugs. We've all partaken in binge drinking the crap out of ourselves and three of us have snorted so much cocaine my face is still numb. So be my guest to stay and answer the uncomfortable questions from the police, but I'm off before we get blamed for this messed-up situation. Who's with me?" I had successfully silenced the bathroom.

Owen looked up at me and said "Samantha darling, you're freaking out."

Too bloody right I was. Explaining the death of an extravagant character like Ulysses, who I'd just met that night, was not on my to-do list today. None of this was. I wasn't supposed to be here.

"I'm with Sam." Jason placed a hand on my shoulder.

I looked to Toni and Sophie, who were looking at each other.

"Should we not call an ambulance before we go? Or at least get some help?" Owen asked as he rose to his feet.

"He's dead. We just need to get as far away from here as possible," Jason said.

Jason's detachment shocked me, but not enough to question it.

Toni climbed out of the bath and held Sophie's hand. "Do you still have the keys to his car?" She asked Owen, who nodded slowly. "Then lets go and just pretend this never happened."

There was no getting away from the fact that pretending the last twenty minutes hadn't happened would be an impossible feat. This was an unforgettable situation that enriched nobody's life except the therapist I would inevitably have to pay to get me to sleep at night. How had we gone from fun and frolics to running away from a dead body in a bathroom? Uly could have already been dead when I was in the bathroom earlier chastising Owen over his sexual exploits. Or maybe he was alive and I could've saved him if I wasn't high on narcotics and lust. It didn't matter now. We were abandoning him in the most undignified position. Ulysses deserved a grander send-off than that. But there was no time, and all five of us bolted through the front door and down the stairs after grabbing what we could of our belongings from the apartment.

"The garage is around the back," Toni shouted through the din of our shoes banging against the metal stairs leading down to the main front door. The sun was now up and its glare made me squint as I stepped outside. I glanced down at my wrist but my watch wasn't there. I'd left it in the bathroom and there was no way I was going back up there. I pulled out my phone; it was already 6.30 a.m. And then it hit me: two deaths in one night and still no real acknowledgement of either.

Death always seemed to make people think about their own mortality. The only certainty in life is death, but funnily enough nobody is ever prepared for it. I needed to get off this bat-shit crazy ride and take a breath.

Chapter Thirteen

Jason decided to take to the wheel despite the fact that he was wildly over the limit like everyone else. In fairness he appeared to be the only person who had his shit together. Sophie pointed out Uly's car. It wasn't a compact little thing but a big beast of a SUV with blacked-out windows. I was fully expecting pink furry dice and a novelty car horn that played Britney Spears, but it was just a plain boring leather interior in pristine condition. It was still early but traffic in the city was already building up. We were hitting every red light but nobody said a word. I flipped down the car's sun visor to shield my eyes from the morning sun. I was up front with Jason. The girls in the back on either side of a forlorn-looking Owen, staring out the windows. I watched in the mirror as he rubbed his mousey hair and then shook his head in disbelief. Right there and then I knew that our decision to flee was the wrong thing to do, but I snapped the sun visor back up and remained silent.

Twenty minutes into the drive I felt like I was going to be sick. I screamed at Jason to pull over, fighting the urge to grab the steering wheel and perform the manoeuvre myself. He finally screeched into a side road and mounted the kerb as I flung open the door and fell to my knees.

I had my first anxiety attack in the vegetable aisle at Tesco. My boss mocked me for eating crap all day long, which I took offense to, while trying to hide my packet of jelly sweets under my notepad. So I needed to prove that I was capable of being a real grown-up who cooks fresh food. But something wasn't sitting right with me that day. I couldn't put my finger on it, but a sense of foreboding was developing inside my chest and it exploded to the surface just as I placed a butternut squash into my basket. Sharp short breaths and sheer panic twisted my insides as I gasped for air. Crouching down on the cold, tiled floor gave me a strange sense of comfort, but to the outsider looking in, I just looked insane. It wasn't until I felt the hand of a shop assistant on my arm that I came back to the present, still straining to focus on what was happening. The feeling of panic levelled out but my mortification and embarrassment sky-rocketed. I ran out of the shop, unable to piece together what had happened.

I put a few hundred metres between me and the supermarket and walked down a quiet residential road. When I collapsed into a seated position on a driveway I noticed I was still carrying a loose red pepper. I juggled it between my clammy hands until it dawned on me that it was stolen goods. I contemplated taking it back but I couldn't face entering the store again. I was left with a feeling of shame and sadness. My heart rate was beating out of rhythm, so I took a few deep breaths to try and regulate it. After a few minutes I felt stable enough to stand and begin the walk home with my stolen red pepper.

The thing is, anxiety didn't seem to discriminate. After furious Internet searches on the subject, an anxiety disorder appeared to play games with everyone and anyone no matter how fucking great you thought your life was. You may have expected to have a truly wonderful day until those feelings of dread and doom decide to ruin it for you.

I had been living with this defect in my head for two years now. Living with it but not coping, and still not sharing it with anyone except my GP. She put me on anti-depressants, which I rebelled against. Funnily enough I didn't feel depressed. I just wanted the anxiety attacks to stop, so I figured I didn't need the prescription pills. I would suppress it with drinking and tearful bouts of self-harming, something that had soothed me ever since I was a teenager. It was the one thing I could control when everything else seemed to be slipping from my grasp. I believed it would ease the conflicting voices in my head, but instead it exacerbated the emotions that feed my self-doubt and loathing. Unfortunately hurting myself was another habit that I wasn't ready to break.

After dramatically throwing myself out of Uly's car, I began going through the motions of an attack. First my hands start twitching, then the palpitations, the sweating, and then the disabling feeling of being unable to breathe. Even though the feeling of nausea would always linger, I never got to the point of throwing up. But this time, with the mix of alcohol, drugs and the image of a dead body in my system, it wasn't long before I was vomiting onto the grass verge next to me. I heard a car door open from behind and then felt a warm hand on me. It was Toni, who was gently rubbing my back. I finally stopped throwing up and fell into her embrace. I was shaking and crying as she held me and rocked me. She may have been somewhat duplicitous in her behaviour, but I needed someone to ground my maddening thoughts, and in this moment it was her.

Chapter Fourteen

By the time I had stopped whinging into Toni's shoulder, everyone was out of the car and sitting on the kerb with me. Jason was smoking a cigarette, Owen had Sophie's head in his lap and Toni still had her arm around me. I wriggled free from her, half embarrassed at my carry-on and half annoyed at whatever went down between Jason and her.

"Is anybody else hungry?" Sophie asked.

"I haven't eaten since my lunch break yesterday," Toni said.

And with that we all decided that we were starving for the first time in hours.

"Lets get out of the city first and stop at the first service station we find." Jason said.

Dragging my heavy body from the pavement into the car caused a dull ache. Although the vehicle was huge, it felt like I had to contort myself to fit into the space. Everything hurt.

None of us were prepared to talk about what had just happened and what we had left back in Soho, and certainly not to discuss what we were doing right now. So I flicked on the radio just loud enough to stifle the atmosphere with music, adverts and impossible competitions where you had to guess the sound. I arched my back and took my phone from my jeans pocket. The battery was flashing red and the time was 7:15 a.m. I felt a shiver like someone had just walked over my grave and I wished I'd remembered to bring my hoodie with me from Uly's apartment.

As road trips go, this one was pretty painful. There were no games of I Spy or Name that Tune, just emotionally charged silence. The only words spoken were requests that I close the window because everyone in the back was freezing, or to change the radio station because Sophie disliked the presenter.

"I dunno what it is," she said, "but she just sounds smug!"

I had no idea how she came to that conclusion. The radio presenter was merely reading out the telephone number for a charity pledge hotline. Maybe it was the way she phonetically spelt out the website that irritated Sophie or maybe she just wanted to take out her anger on someone or anyone.

We were heading in a straight line on the motorway, just coasting along. I was impressed with Jason's driving skills but still secretly shitting myself at the prospect of being stopped for driving a billion times over the limit. We hadn't slept in nearly twenty-four hours, so if the police didn't get to us first, sleep-deprivation would. Sailing past various junctions and confusing lane merges confirmed my reluctance to ever learn to drive. I saw a sign for a Wimpy fast-food restaurant and a petrol station. I then lowered the volume of the radio and tried to concentrate on finding the correct exit. Jason dropped us off at the entrance to the tired looking restaurant as he went to fill up the car with petrol. For a split second, as the four of us unfolded ourselves and got out of the car, I thought Jason would drive off and leave us there. But it was too late now and I was almost 90 per cent sure my friend wouldn't do that.

Five coffees, three bacon sandwiches and two pieces of toast were ordered and haphazardly thrown onto the ketchup-stained table we were huddled around. Jason still hadn't arrived but I bought him a coffee all the same.

"How do you think he's holding up?" Owen asked me after pulling a disgusted face from the rancid bitter coffee.

"Well, we're all not holding up!" Sophie said, irritated again.

"Yeah, but Jason also found out that his dad died yesterday. So if this was a competition, which I'm fully aware it's not, Jason would win at this falling-apart game right now." I didn't mean to snap at her but it was slowly dawning on me that befriending Toni and Sophie was an utterly shite idea. If I hadn't been so willing to just go with the flow and naively follow my fanny flutter in the direction of an exotic Portuguese lady, we would not be in this disastrous situation.

Sophie lowered her head and mumbled, "Well, I didn't know that," and took a bite of her toasted sandwich.

"This is *louco!*" Toni slammed both hands down onto the table, which caught the attention of two builders in high-viz jackets behind us. "Uly was my friend. We have just left my friend behind like filthy cowards and stolen his car! What are we? Animals? We must go back!" A tear rolled down her cheek, leaving a track in her make-up. I instinctively reached across the table to hold her hand.

"We just panicked and needed some perspective," I said, "But I agree. We need to get back and sort this mess out."

I offered a half-smile to the table; Owen and Sophie nodded in agreement. Toni squeezed my hand and I squeezed it back three times. It was something my friend and I used to do back at school before we became strangers. Three squeezes was our signal that everything would be okay even when we knew deep down that it probably wouldn't be okay at all.

"You guys finish your fabulous breakfasts," I said in a jovial sarcastic tone, "and I'll go and find Jason. We need to get back to the city."

I picked up his now lukewarm coffee and headed back out to the main entrance.

"Here, take this." Sophie followed me to the door and handed me her jacket. "It's freezing outside."

I accepted with a tired grateful smile. Now, where the hell was this boy?

Chapter Fifteen

I had paced across the car park twice already and there were no cars like Uly's on the petrol station's forecourt. I headed back on myself and rubbed my eyes. This no-sleep thing was starting to sap my energy and the third succession of dry heaving told me that my full-blown hangover was only moments away. I edged my phone out of my pocket. It had just 4 per cent charge remaining but I had to call him. I didn't expect him to pick up, so I was surprised when the phone connected with a click.

"Where the fudge are you J?"

"Turn around, you big idiot. I'm right here!"

I turned and scanned the cars again to see Jason sat in the ginormous car, waving at me. I could have sworn he wasn't there before. I went to shout "Stupid prick" down the phone but I got as far as "You stupid pr– " before my phone died.

Thank the baby Jesus the heating was on as I saddled up next to Jason. The coffee I was clutching was now stone cold, so I placed it in the cup holder, admitting defeat.

"Hey, listen, I tried but you never came back!"

He simply smiled indifferently like he had when I met him in the bar so many hours before.

Ignoring his spaced-out attitude I said, "We've decided to go back to the city and sort this madness out. We're running away from something that wasn't even our fault to begin with, so we need to stop the lunacy post haste!"

Throwing a post haste at the end of any sentence usually made Jason giggle at the intentional Shakespearean dramatics of it all. But this time he just kept staring out the windscreen.

"J, I know the past night has been super-rough for you more than anyone, and I know we agreed not to talk about it, but I would rather you talk to me because I don't think I can cope listening to you ruin another perfectly fine Willy Mason song again!"

He turned toward me, laughed out loud and then rested his head on the steering wheel.

"How have we got here Sam?" It was now my turn to gaze out the window trying to recall how this night spiralled into one big epic meltdown.

Jason began to scratch, agitated at the stubble on his face.

"If I hadn't called you to come and meet me, we wouldn't be running away from a dead man in Soho right now. I just wanted a distraction. I needed to not think. I'm so sorry, Sam, for everything, including Toni. I knew you liked her but my brain didn't communicate with my dick until it was too late! Nothing good has come out of this degenerate event."

I was listening to his mini-monologue but I couldn't look at him. Not because I was mad at him for Toni, which in hindsight was insignificant in the grand scheme of things, but because I couldn't handle him crying on me. This was a first for our friendship and I wasn't equipped.

"I'm pretty sure that life isn't meant to be this hard." I began my own unabridged soliloquy. "The sun rises in the morning and sets in the evening, and it is us who dick around with that goes on in between. Things don't have to be this serious or catastrophic. We are the ones who over-complicate a very simple straightforward process." I sighed heavily. Why was it so hard? But that's just life. We make it up as we go along, and as we get older, we all just wing it and pray that it will all make sense in the end.

"I'm also fully convinced that we create our own drama. Taking a dead stranger's car and driving it out of the city is drama we all forged out of fear and rash decision-making. And we need to put it right. J, I'm so tired of making stupid mistakes and not realising we've fucked up until we're sat in a stationary car mouthing the words *Oh bollocks!* Please lets get off this bloody hamster wheel, because it's making me sick."

Jason delicately placed his hand on my thigh and rested it there. I think that was the first time he had touched my leg with real sincerity, without a trace of the flirting and sexual innuendos he was prone to. I could hear him sniffle but I still refused to break off my staring match with the empty parking space opposite us. After a short pause that seemed like an awkward decade, he turned the radio on and Abba's "Dancing Queen" came through the speakers.

"Do you fancy a dance?" Jason asked rubbing his eyes. He had already whacked the volume up and was now opening the door.

"What, right now?"

Of course he meant right now. Jason laughed and stood to the side of the car doing the most ridiculous dance to the campest song in the world. I jumped out of the car and ran around to meet him. What followed was an array of dance moves ripped straight from the manual *How to Dance like Your Dad at a Wedding*.

We were glorious, ungraceful creatures dancing like nobody was watching at a service-station car park. People were watching but we just didn't care. We owned the song with its pop riffs and synthesised keyboard. And if they'd had the night we had, they too would be thrusting their groin in a provocative manner like any slutty dancing queen would! Jason grabbed my waist and took the lead in a lively tango-style routine that was hilariously out of time with the music. I kept throwing my head back and stopping to allow for bouts of laughter. There was always something about dancing for me. It intensified all my senses and juiced up my happy levels. In that service-station car park, gliding through every improvised step with the poise of a euthanized ape, I felt an instant gratifying high. It was natural and positive. My exhaustion disappeared as I threw the most peculiar shapes to a passing coachload of schoolkids.

Jason twirled me around and dipped me clumsily a few times before he lost his balance and almost fell. We both cracked up laughing and continued to enjoy the buzz of energy until the song faded into an advert for a furniture sale. The erratic dancing and laughter allowed us both to disconnect from the moment and get back to grassroots. We needed to return to what we knew and loved – shedding the serious and indulging the fun. One full minute of what can only be described as interpretive dance to high energy Swedish pop was our way of sticking up the middle finger to what had passed and what would surely come.

Chapter Sixteen

It was clear what had been decided in our absence as soon as Jason and I met with the others back in Wimpy's. In fairness none of us had slept for what seemed like an eternity and I was fairly confident my post-traumatic stress would kick in any moment now – something I was hugely unprepared for.

"There's a B&B just across the way!" Sophie said, asking a question through a statement. "We should just book a couple of rooms, have a little sleep and then head back. And besides, driving now would be far too dangerous."

Funny how it was now considered dangerous to drive when we all fully supported Jason taking the wheel after he had just stuffed a gram of coke up his nose and downed a litre of whiskey. A short snooze was a necessity for all of us, but whether we'd be able to sleep would be another thing altogether.

Entering the foyer of the B&B, we were met at the front desk by an old woman, possibly in her seventies, wearing a grease-stained tabard and clutching a feather duster. By *front desk* I mean a small coffee table with a giant bowl of potpourri in the middle. She seemed to hesitate to check availability, until Jason laid his credit card down. I could make no financial contribution as I had spent my last tenner on the disgusting coffee and the toast I didn't eat. The lady perked up instantly at the sight of the plastic, and went to fetch our keys.

Sophie and Owen walked ahead through the narrow hallway. Jason quickened his pace to overtake Toni and me. I could see what he was doing and I was cringing inside.

"So, us three in this room and you and Toni in that one." Jason pointed out the rooms as we came to a junction in the hallway. He threw a key at me. I went to protest but he had already entered his room with the others.

"I'm the only one who has enough charge on my phone, so I'll set the alarm and wake you all up in two hours max. So power-nap to your hearts' content, you little shits!" And with a smirk, Jason turned and slammed the door.

Toni and I were left on our own. I had no energy to over-analyse this situation, so I just opened the door to our room and stepped inside.

The room was reminiscent of my nan's living room circa 1986. Mint-green carpet and peach wallpaper on the walls, probably inspired by an English meadow. The décor was harsh on our eyes but was equally the most inoffensive environment I had been in in the last twenty-four hours. There was a sense of home about it, even down to the smell of lavender-scented mothballs hanging in the single wardrobe, which balanced precariously on three legs. In the middle of the room stood one double bed, more potpourri and two girls far too exhausted to embrace this awkward scenario. I climbed on top of the bed, lay on my back and sighed deeply. Toni lay down next to me and rolled over on her side to face me. Bollocks! She wanted chats and I was all out of conversation.

"Are we okay, Sam?"

I sighed again but still refused to face her.

"Yes, we're fine." I was totally lying. "There's just so much going on right now that I really want to switch off for a moment without having to engage in another chat about our feelings. There's been enough drama for one day!"

She shuffled and rolled her body away from me, visibly upset, and said, "Okay, well, I'm sorry I asked."

I was the only person causing a spectacle at this stage, so I needed to stop. I shifted my body up on the bed so I was sitting against the headboard. As I looked across at Toni I could see the tattoo on her arm again.

"What does your tattoo say?" I enquired, half curious and half trying to break the icy silence I had just created.

"*Até ao lavar dos cestos é vindima.* Loosely translated, in English it means 'Never say die'. I got it when I was sixteen with a bunch of school friends. I was, how you say, a rebel without a clue!" Toni spoke into the wall she was facing still too stubborn to give me eye contact.

I began to laugh out loud and it was this that made her face me.

"I'm sorry! I don't mean to sound rude, but you basically have a Goonies tattoo on you!"

She looked at me, confused, and then spoke the blasphemous words, "What is this Goonies?"

I immediately stopped laughing and stared back at her in disbelief. "What's *The Goonies*? Only one of the greatest eighties movies in the history of the world ever! Their motto is 'Goonies never say die' just like your tattoo!"

"Does this make my tattoo ridiculous to you?" Toni was clearly offended and my laughing was ill timed.

"No, no, not at all. It's one of my favourite films. We'll have to watch it some day." I managed to recover from my poor decision to laugh in the girl's face, and her pissed-off expression relaxed.

"I'd like that very much," she said, now smiling.

Now, if we were on the set of a romantic black and white film, I probably would've been playing the help or incarcerated for having a sassy mouth and not being Caucasian. But if Toni and I were the leads, this would've been the part where I swept her up in a dramatic fashion and kissed her in a passionate but awkward tryst resulting in whiplash or some sort of repetitive strain injury. But this was real life, and a rundown B&B at a service station wasn't my idea of romance. Plus only three hours previously she had been knee deep in Jason's manly embrace and herpe-fied penis. Granted I had no idea if he had herpes, but it was comforting that there would be consequences to their promiscuity, even if just in my imagination. Toni moved closer to me and formed the foetal position into the side of my body. It caught me off guard, but in that moment it was welcome. I tentatively placed my arm around her back and rested my head onto the headboard. I wanted to sleep but my mind was having an illegal rave and I could hear the irregular beat of my own pulse in my ear. I was too nervous to close my eyes because I

Chapter Seventeen

The first nightmare I can recall having was when I was about six years old. I was walking through my local town centre with my mother, holding her hand. As we turned into a cobbled side road, a waxy, green, chubby alien jumped out from a hidden doorway. My mother simply stood there, still holding my hand, as the expressionless alien approached me. I didn't scream, because in dreams carry-on like running or calling for help is completely ineffective. If you're in trouble in your subconscious, then your likelihood of survival is as high as that of the black best friend in every teen horror movie, ever. If you're going to get caught, then so be it! The overweight alien extended a gnarly finger and proceeded to poke me really hard in my ear. The pain was excruciating and I woke from my nightmare in sweat and tears. I refused to watch the film *E.T.* on my own again.

That day in the B&B I knew it was only a matter of time before I would be in a coma-like sleep, with a host of dead bodies lying in vintage bathtubs. I tried to fight the fatigue but I soon slipped into a world of zombified Uly's. Everywhere I turned I was faced with a sad and dejected Uly with those eyes rolled back in his head and his pale lips saying over and over, "But Samantha, I thought we were friends?" I could feel anger burning in the pit of my stomach as I tried to escape avoiding his questioning. In the distance I could see the guys – Toni, Sophie,

Jason and Owen – drinking in The Cellar Door and laughing hysterically without me. I was waving frantically, trying to get their attention, but nobody noticed me. Jason and Toni stood up and began passionately kissing as Sophie and Owen continued laughing and clinking their glasses together. I started to run, aware that another monstrous Uly was coming after me, but my legs wouldn't move. I tried to speed up, but after every futile sprint forward, I was dragged back. The heat of anger in my stomach was now replaced by an acute fear in my chest as Ulysses, dressed in drag and an elaborate Native American headdress, shoved me hard in my back. I was falling forward head first into the path of a double-decker bus, with no control over my body and nobody there to save me.

I woke up abruptly, my T-shirt sticking to my back with sweat. After the panic of the freakish dream faded, it was the blinking into darkness that frightened me next. That ten-seconds of pure disorientation when you wake up in a foreign environment hit me with flash of terror. I jumped out of bed unaware of my surroundings and of who was asleep in the bed next to me. I extended my arms in front of me trying to steady myself and feel my way to the window. I then squinted through the net curtain trying to process the fact that the streetlights were on. Straightening up from my hunchbacked, sleepy posture, the realisation sunk in and I felt the colour drain from my face. This was definitely not the two-hour powernap we had planned and we all were most definitely screwed.

I threw on the room lights, knocking over the bowl of potpourri in the process and shouted at Toni to get up. She flailed around for a moment and took a short sharp breath, shocked to see my face. We needed to get the hell out of there. "I'll go get the others." My voice sounded rough and deep as if I had digested Barry White's greatest hits on vinyl.

"What time is it?" Toni asked with a wobble in her voice. I automatically looked at my wrist, forgetting I had lost my watch, and then grabbed my phone from my pocket, overlooking the fact that the battery had died hours ago.

"I have no idea. All I know is that we went to sleep in daylight and now it's dark!" And with that I flew out of the door to wake the others.

If the incessant banging on the door didn't wake them, my dull screaming would've done the trick. There was movement inside and then a giant crash, followed by Owen reeling off a list of expletives. He opened the door and rubbed his eyes.

"What's happening?" He blurted out, still dazed and confused. "I just walked into the bloody dressing table!"

I barged past him and flicked on the room light. Sophie was starfished across the double bed and Jason was in the floral armchair by the window. I ran over to Jason and shook him harder than I probably should have, but it was nothing more than he deserved.

"Why didn't you wake us? What happened to the alarm? We've slept for too long. We need to let someone know about Uly!" Jason, terrified that I might throw a punch or the armchair at his head, scurried to find his phone. He had placed it on the dressing table and so it was now lying on the floor after Owen had collided with the furniture. Toni arrived and picked up the phone. "It's 8.23 p.m.," she said, "and telling someone about Uly is no longer necessary."

Toni turned on the small TV in the corner of the room and found a news bulletin. She fiddled with the coat-hanger aerial until the reception improved just enough for us to read the headline: "London stockbroker found dead at home." The newsreader spoke to the camera as a photo of Uly flashed up on the screen. If it wasn't for the perfectly groomed eyebrows and the cheeky grin, I wouldn't have recognised the corporate-looking man in the suit as Uly. The man I met hours ago was flamboyant and loud, dressed in clothing snug enough for a Ken doll. The guy in the picture was just another affluent Londoner with too much gel in his hair. Sophie, now fully awake, gasped in horror behind me.

"Police are on the lookout for a missing vehicle belonging to the deceased. They are treating it as suspicious and would like to speak to anyone who may have any information."

I felt a sick feeling in the pit of my stomach again and wanted to vomit right there and then.

Jason backed further and further away from the TV as if every word spoken by the newsreader was attacking him. He reversed into the armchair and lowered himself back into it. I had only been associated with the criminal underworld twice previously. Once with the stolen red pepper from Tesco, and another time when a friend decided to shoplift a pencil eraser from our local stationery shop. I thought we were genuinely looking for back-to-school supplies and not staging a heist. I wanted no part of it and declined to steal the accompanying pencil sharpener as my friend suggested.

"Well if you're not going to take anything, then at least distract the old man behind the till for me," my friend whispered through gritted teeth.

So this was what peer pressure felt like. I remember the teachers in our personal and social health care classes talking about this form of bullying. Nevertheless, I found myself asking the shopkeeper if he could check in the storeroom for a book of twelve first class stamps. As soon as his back was turned my friend and I ran like the wind. When she knocked for me the next day to ask me out to play, I hid in my room and made my mum lie and tell her I wasn't feeling well. Running away from the scene of a crime was clearly a thing of mine.

Chapter Eighteen

The TV was eventually switched off and the five of us were stunned into silence again. It was like a giant game of snakes and ladders. We had progressed three squares forward, advanced up a ladder, rolled again, moved one square forward to then land on a snake that had sent us crashing down to the start again. If there were ever an opportune time to drop to my knees in a Platoon death-scene style and scream "Why?" at the top of my lungs, now was it. It was easy to place the blame on Jason for not waking us all up like he had promised, but the fact of the matter was that we had all contributed to this saga.

"But we were coming back," Owen muttered. "And now we're fucking fugitives up on theft, and potentially murder, charges!"

Nobody spoke; we all knew what Owen said was the truth. My stomach churned. We'd never be able to talk ourselves out of this predicament because it was already far too ludicrous to be believable.

"We need to get back to the city, and no more diversions. Let's just get out of here and hand ourselves in." Sophie stood up with enough assertiveness to make us all follow her lead. We had to go back and explain this mess.

With a pain in my head and an urgent purposeful walk, we headed towards the foyer of the B&B. The old lady in the tabard was nowhere to be seen, even after Toni's ringing of the bell incessantly for two minutes.

"Eh, Toni, the bell thing really isn't doing much," Jason said in an attempt to get her to stop.

Toni gave him a death stare and pressed the bell one more time.

"Do we really need to officially checkout?" I asked, trying to understand the need for the hold up. "The old lady already took the payment, so can we not just leave?"

"You're absolutely right, Samantha," Owen said, grabbing a pen and paper from the table. "I'll just write her a little note so she knows we left already."

The note read: "Thanks for your top-notch hospitality. You were very kind! Our rooms were very comfortable and homely. The décor, however, could do with some modernisation and more complementary essentials in the bathroom would have been handy. Have a lovely day! From the party of five in rooms 112 and 114." And with that unnecessary review, we left.

Owen nominated himself to drive by simply taking the keys from Jason. Jason sat up front and the girls and I fell into the back seats. Although it was freezing, I wound down the window just enough so I could breathe fresh air and hopefully prevent another anxiety attack. No diversions this time, just like Sophie had said. We need to get from A to B without complicating matters with C and D or any other letters of the alphabet.

Toni sat in the middle with her head rested on Sophie's shoulder. "What are we going to tell the police?" she asked.

"The truth," Jason said, staring off into the night.

"We messed up, guys," I said, "but we're going to make it right. Goonies never say die, remember!" I ended with a ridiculous fist pump into the air and a nervous laugh. My attempt at a pep talk was as potent as erectile dysfunction. I could see Owen smile sympathetically in the mirror, but it would have been as inappropriate to laugh out loud as it was to make a joke in the first place. Toni reached out and squeezed my hand three times. She remembered.

Jason fiddled with the radio and the DJ announced that it was 8.35 p.m. I started to recognise landmarks, so I knew we were getting closer into town. The vivid lights can be quite eye-watering when you're entering the city after being in the asshole of nowhere for a few hours. My favourite light show was the neon ballet of Piccadilly Circus that still excited me as much as it had done when I was a child. The buses chugging slowly around the roundabout, pedestrians wrestling each other in a quest to get everywhere and anywhere, and the ginormous Coca-Cola sign, the grandmaster of London iconography. It was my favourite tourist spot and it made the city feel magical and romantic after sunset.

I noticed that Owen was looking in his rear-view mirror more often than he had for the past half an hour or so of driving. Something had caught his attention and this in turn piqued my interest. "Is that a police car behind us?"

We all whipped our necks around to see if we could spot what Owen had. I was fully prepared to dismiss his paranoia and blame the city's neon jungle, but of course not tonight. Not on a night when trying to right a wrong was riddled with complications. The flashing blue lights were clearly visible, as were the full beam headlights instructing us to pull over. It was the first time that day when I thought, "If I make it out alive, my parents are just going to kill me anyway."

Chapter Nineteen

Owen pulled into the nearest lay-by and two police cars stopped behind us. On a scale of one to shit your pants, I was close to the soiled-underwear end of the scale.

"Everyone just relax and stay calm," Owen whispered. "Let's just see what they want first, before we reveal all."

Two officers approached the driver's side as Owen pressed the button to lower the window.

"Is everything okay?" Owen shouted out to them in a high-pitched panicked voice that screamed *I'm guilty! Take me to jail!* One of the officers who appeared stretched like a beanpole, crouched over ever so slightly to peer into the car with a flashlight.

"We have reason to believe that this vehicle has been stolen. Can you all please step out of the car. I'll need to see a driver's licence." That was it. There was no use in staying calm or keeping quiet. Cue full-blown internal hysteria.

We got out of the car and sat at the edge of the lay-by, watching three of the four police officers search the vehicle for who knows what. I still had nothing warmer than my T-shirt to wear, so I didn't know if I was shivering because of nerves or the Baltic temperature. I glazed over, lay back and started counting the stars and a few low-flying planes. It was totally unfitting for the moment I was in, but I could feel my heart rate rising and I needed to occupy myself somehow. When I was a kid I would sit in the back of the car and pretend an imaginary man was running beside me on the pavement. Every time there was a break in the path, I would envisage this man leaping the entire distance, often three houses wide, and landing effortlessly as soon as the path became continuous and safe for him to run again. I used to suffer from motion sickness and it was the only way I could distract myself so I wouldn't throw up. Make-believe distractions always made me feel safe. Lying there on the edge of a cold lay-by was how I imagined death would be – calm and silent, with nothing but stars and daydreams to occupy my thoughts. This is how I wanted it to be for now and always.

"Samantha!" My name filtered through to my brain and I was yanked back into the moment. Owen had one of my arms and was trying to pull me to my feet. He whispered, "You need to focus and stop making a show of me!"

Two of the police officers stood before us as I clambered to my feet.

"Where are the guys?" I enquired looking over my shoulders and realising that only one police car remained.

Speaking through a grimace Owen said, "They went in the other car, remember? We'll follow them to the station in this one."

One of the officers placed a hand on my shoulder and asked, "Are you all right, love?"

I shrugged his hand off and nodded my head. I hate when strangers address me as *love* or *sweetheart*, or when random taxi

drivers greet me with *All right, treacle!* It made me feel
subservient and damsel-in-distress-esque when I was neither.
We walked past Uly's car and were calmly guided into the back
of the police car. I was fully expecting handcuffs and police
brutality, but there was no drama. Owen went to hold my hand
and I flinched, unprepared for the contact. He released his grip
just before I could give it a squeeze.

"What's happening with you?" Owen asked, annoyed.

I could see the officer in the passenger seat watching us.
"Nothing," I lied.

"It'll be okay. We just have to answer a few questions about
the party and explain what happened. It's all routine stuff." Now
Owen was lying, or maybe he was just daring to believe that
everything really would be okay. He appeared to have no idea
how complicated this could get, and the fact that we were being
escorted to a police station didn't bode well for anyone. One of
my biggest fears, born from watching too many Hollywood
movies, was to be arrested for something I didn't do. I would be
thrown into jail with no way to prove my innocence and no
money to hire a hot-headed, inexperienced lawyer like Tom
Cruise just so I could scream in the courtroom, "YOU CAN'T
HANDLE THE TRUTH!"

But I had done something wrong. I was the one who bullied
everyone into leaving Uly's apartment without reporting it in the
first place. If only we had just called someone like Owen had
wanted. If only we hadn't run like idiots. If only we hadn't fallen

asleep. Unfortunately *3 x if only* in the back of a police car amounted to jack shit.

I pondered the thought of the one phone call they had to offer us, as depicted in every cop movie ever. The sensible choice would be my parents, who would bail me out of this nightmare in a heartbeat. However, there would be a clause attached to this ticket to freedom that would involve something along the lines of moving back home, never talking about it ever again, and breaking connection to the homosexual lifestyle. Because of course that was the main reason behind my poor decision-making skills – my perverse love of the clitoris.

Or I could save the call and be a real grown-up who handles my own chaos. I'm sure the horror of a prison sentence would be an interesting learning curve or at least something to tell the grandchildren. I could just embrace the fact that I was a criminal who needed to be punished and relish the thought of a prison sentence over the wrath my parents. The polyester prison outfits would do nothing to enhance my oblong torso, and yes, I probably would be attacked by a thuggish inmate who had fashioned a toothbrush, a sanitary towel and a hairclip into a stabbing device. But being the prison wife of some crazy lesbian called Papi, who had a glass eye and scar on her face nobody dared talk about, didn't *really* sound so bad.

Chapter Twenty

She handed me a plastic cup of water and told me to relax. Her voice had all the sentiment of a pissed-off nurse instructing me to relax during a smear test. The walls were exposed brickwork, but the funky dog-eared carpet scuppered any hope of the room ever featuring in an interior design magazine. I lowered the cup from my chapped lips and noticed my hands were shaking. Sitting across from a female law-enforcer was terrifying. She looked like one of my friends' mothers wearing a power suit with fierce shoulder pads. The kind of mum who would pick us up from netball practice and then cook us chicken nuggets, chips and beans for tea. I began to miss my mum. Despite all that was occurring I still craved her approval and the look that said, *You're a complete ass, but I still love you.* The detective broke my thoughts with a loud rustle of her papers. Her lips were thin and she pursed them as if she was constantly puffing on menthol cigarettes. "Now, just start at the beginning," she said. She then spoke into the tape recorder and during the rehearsed intro she noted the time. It was 9.48 p.m.

I spoke as eloquently as I possibly could with a voice that trembled, just to demonstrate that I was somewhat educated and not an illiterate scumbag. The detective inspector seemed pleasant enough, but she interrupted often with obvious questions that required long answers.

"So why were you in the bathroom with the others?" She queried.

"I just said! I needed the toilet! Why else would I go?!" I said with a little too much insolence. I needed to calm down and tuck my attitude in. The lack of food, intermittent nightmare-filled sleep and thoughts of the unglamorous world of prison were thoroughly kicking my ass, but I had to control my feisty mouth. As I spoke about the party, the bathroom, the idiotic running away, the falling asleep and the finally getting caught, the officer broke in with a question that stumped me. "You all had mobile phones on you, am I correct?"

I nodded my head, still confused at what she was getting at. "Yes."

"So why did nobody think to call the police?"

I instantly went to feel for my phone in my pocket out of nerves and out of habit. I had a mini heart attack when I couldn't find it, and then I remembered I had handed it in when we arrived at the station. Moments before we were all split up and sent into separate rooms to be questioned. If we had just called the police from the start, before my battery died, and reported Uly's death, this wouldn't have escalated into the farce it was. But we had all scared ourselves into thinking we had a hand in Uly's untimely death, and the further away from the problem we got the better. After all, we were all enjoying the fast-paced lifestyle of drink, drugs and inappropriate sexual favours. We were all in it together. So, in my irrational mind, we were all inescapably linked to Uly's downfall. It was our fault. In answer to the detective's question I simply said, "I don't know. I just panicked. I wasn't thinking." I had never felt so weak and small in my life. The guilt was itching away at me like a rash. She looked down to write in her notepad.

"Did we kill Ulysses?" I asked.

The detective looked up from her notepad and parted her lips. "No. No, Samantha, you didn't." A male uniformed officer entered the room, whispered something inaudible into her ear and placed a folder on the table. She turned to say thank you and he left.

"So what happened to him?" I asked. She ignored me for a few uncomfortable seconds as she flicked through the new folder. She then placed her biro on the table and clasped her hands together in front of her. It was the perfect pose, often adopted by teachers at parents' evening when they're about to say what an unruly shit their child was. I swallowed hard on whatever saliva I had in my dry mouth and awaited her response.

"We received the lab reports from the toxicology department on Mr Ulysses Costas. There were high levels of the chemical diamorphine found in his body. It would seem that he died of a heroin overdose. It's still inconclusive as to whether this was accidental or not."

The words stung me like a thousand honeybees willing to sacrifice their life just to teach me a lesson. I managed only an okay in reply.

"Whatever happened at this party, I am sure you and your friends were unaware of Mr Costas' intentions. However, the matter of stealing a vehicle and leaving the scene of the crime is worrying. Fines will be issued to your friends for driving a car without the appropriate insurance." Her lips were pursed harder than before. "But I am confident that you all acted out of inexperience, immaturity and downright stupidity. The only redeeming fact is that you were coming back, which suggests you were trying, albeit badly, to undo your mess."

She leaned over to the tape recorder, mumbled some words, looked at her watch and said, "Interview terminated at 10.28 p.m."

So that was it. It was over. I peeled myself out of the chair and followed her out of the room.

"So, urmm, so is that everything?" I stuttered.

She turned to directly face me, narrowed her eyes and said, "Yes, for now."

And with that she coolly walked out of sight, down a corridor. I collected my phone and my wallet, the only items I had with me. Then the same male officer who had entered the room earlier handed me my hoodie.

"How did you know this was mine?" I asked, delighted to see it.

"It was found at the apartment and it has your employment photo ID in one of the pockets."

Of course! I had completely forgotten.

When I reached the station's front desk, nobody was there. Oh God, had one of them been charged? Did Jason supply the heroin? Sophie had been suspicious and twitchy. Did Toni also lead Uly on just to get out of paying rent? Was Uly's party just a grand cover up of a drug syndicate for gay men? And did the fact that Owen "interfered" with Uly mean he was a prime suspect? I couldn't cope. I needed air. Right now. I zipped up my hoodie and pushed the heavy double doors to exit the building. Sat on the steps were Jason, Owen, Toni and Sophie. Sophie ran over to me and hugged me so hard it knocked me back. Sophie, the girl who didn't do hugs or any form of sentiment, just kept on squeezing me. My friends were just fine.

Chapter Twenty-One

Before the doors of the Tube opened at Tottenham Court Road, it was decided we would all go home and process the last twenty-four hours. We needed time, space, food and sleep in our own beds. But as the doors opened, we all looked at each other and silently agreed to get off. We sprang out of our seats and jumped free as the familiar voice bellowed "Please mind the gap" through the carriages. Rejuvenated, we ran through the station and up the escalators. I never walked up the escalators, never mind ran. The image of being sucked under the machine like a shiny wellington boot was far too real for me, as well as the shame for needing a defibrillator once I got to the top as a result of being so unfit. Tonight, though, I was fresh-faced and nimble on my feet, and I would run to the summit just because I could.

Making our way into Soho, it was apparent that nothing had changed. The pavements were still damp and the streets were alive with dark figures wrapped up in coats, scarves, skinny jeans and the odd tourist on holiday, unaware that they had just walked into the gay Mecca of the city. The only noticeable change was that the gay community was down one more member, Ulysses. Standing at the threshold to The Cellar Door I felt a strong rush of familiarity. I was grabbed again by the same feeling of trepidation that rocked me when I'd stood there the day before.

"I'll be in in a minute," Jason said as he lit up a cigarette and blew the smoke away from us.

I nodded and followed the others in.

This time nobody was sitting at our table. Toni asked us what we wanted to drink and headed over to the bar to speak to one of her colleagues. I ordered an orange juice because alcohol seemed oddly unnecessary right now.

"So how are we doing?" Owen asked. There was a strange atmosphere and we all were feeding it with awkward silences and sideway glances.

"I feel relieved, hungry, furious, sad and still hungry!" Sophie said, making larger-than-life hand movements.

Owen chuckled and I joined in. I think he had a new friend in Sophie. The type of girl who would drink mimosas with him on a Sunday afternoon, give her opinion on everything whether he asked for it or not and be outraged that nobody was giving her enough attention.

I excused myself and headed to the toilets. I bolted the door to the dingy cubicle and leant both hands against the inside of the partition. I didn't have the energy to weep as my body felt knotted with intense pressurised despair that would potentially explode any minute. My skin didn't feel like my own. It felt itchy and unclean as if a full-body chemical peel was the only way to wash away the grime. I looked up at the cubicle door and began to read the "highbrow" graffiti. Some were political –

"Fuck the government!" – and the rest consisted of drawings of genitalia, and powerful messages such as "Toy Story 2 was only OK." I chuckled to myself at the genius absurdity of this and considered the high number of people who carried marker pens with them to the toilet. It was time to leave.

When I stepped out of the stall it was the first time since Uly's apartment that I had time to acknowledge the mess of me in the mirror. I fingered through my curls, trying to massage life back into my locks. My hair had lost all shape and volume and my eyes were red from exhaustion. With a look of defeat, I splashed some water onto my face as if a baptism of tap H2O would cleanse my soul of the events of the last twenty-four hours. It would take more than water to awaken something inside that I had now acknowledged to be dead. Straightening up and stretching my spine with a creak, I gave my T-shirt a good deep sniff and recoiled in disgust. I certainly wasn't winning any beauty contests tonight.

Toni finally came over with our drinks as I joined the table, and my orange juice looked and smelled suspiciously like a vodka and coke.

"Sorry, Sam, but we're fresh out of oranges so I had to improvise!" She then flashed me a smile like the one she gave me on our first meeting. I theatrically shrugged my shoulders and raised my glass in the air. "To Ulysses." And with that, the four of us clinked our glasses and silently took the first sip of our beverages.

I had assumed the police officer had informed everyone about Uly's death, even though none of us talked about the details of our interrogation. The only thing we collectively knew and had to take responsibility for was the £300 fixed fine for driving a car without the correct insurance. Apart from that, it would never be discussed again, because at this point there really wasn't anything left to say.

"So did you find out what happened to Jason's dad?" Owen asked me as he took another swig of his pint. I had forgotten. After everything that had happened, I still had no idea about the event that brought us all together last night. As if on cue, Jason strode through the door. I still needed to speak to him, and the bar he'd imposed on the topic of his dad's death had to be lifted.

Chapter Twenty-Two

Sometimes when I was having one of my bad days, I just couldn't help it. I would try and talk myself out of it but it was no use. There was a physical pain inside my heart and head and I just wanted to gouge it out with a blunt instrument. When I was a teenager I would often curl up on the floor in my bedroom, hoping that if I could hold my breath, it all would stop. But my mother knocking on the door and yelling that my dinner was on the table would inevitably interrupt my Zen. I would shout that I wasn't hungry, even though the delicious smells had wafted upstairs and lodged themselves in my nostrils.

The ceiling of my childhood bedroom had swirly patterns in the plaster. I would lie very still on my back and make out funny faces, people with big noses or elongated limbs. It was like I had discovered my very own LSD experience! If I crossed my eyes and refocused, I could sometimes make those faces come to life. One time I stared too hard and a scary-looking clown with a freakish smile bore down on me, at which point I jumped up, scared shitless, and looked for something else to distract myself.

I was only fifteen but I knew something set me apart from the other girls. I didn't find joy in the boy band "hunks of burning love", but I adorned my bedroom walls with their oiled-up torsos all the same. I was a likeable kid and all my close friends were boys. When my maths teacher moved me to a table of all girls one day because I was laughing too loudly with the lads at the back of the class, I was devastated. It was a horrible punishment. I had nothing in common with them, and their chats about which boys they fancied that week infuriated me. It was the first time in weeks that I was in such close proximity to my ex-best friend, who was now sat adjacent to me. I scowled the whole way through that maths lesson and spent my time scratching a smiley face into the back of my calculator with a compass. My ex-best friend stared into her textbook, refusing to glance in my direction. I'd noticed her looking at me in assembly earlier that morning, but she didn't dare show any interest in me now.

"Sam, which one is your boyfriend?" One of the girls opposite said, giggling at me and implying that one of my boy friends was a love interest. The thought of that made my skin crawl even more than their idle gossip.

"I don't have a boyfriend," I said gruffly, unable to maintain any eye contact. This answer encouraged more giggling.

"What are you, a lesbian or something?"

The laughter erupted as the table of girls fell about themselves throwing each other congratulatory looks. My ex-best friend looked up and hesitated as if she was going to intervene on my behalf, but she just remained still and began to laugh with rest of the coven. I didn't have a witty comeback, so I remained silent and simply dug the compass deeper into my calculator.

The school bell rang out and I quickly gathered up my books and threw them into my bag. I needed to get away from the bad vibes. I ran into the nearest toilets like a dramatic Disney princess and bolted the door before I began to cry into the sleeve of my starchy and restrictive blazer. *No matter what, the enemy must never see you cry*, I repeated over in my mind. I didn't want anyone to know how upset I was. I didn't want to appear weak and vulnerable, as I figured that would only encourage the teasing and the question marks chasing me around. If I could have my moment alone and suppress the toxic emotions until home time, then everything would be okay.

After a few minutes I composed myself and unlocked the door. Standing by the hand basins was my ex-best friend staring back at me as I wiped my eyes.

"Are you okay?" She asked.

I shrugged my shoulders and walked over to the sinks to wash my hands.

"I didn't tell them, ya know … that you, ya know … that you're gay."

I closed my eyes at the pain of hearing that taboo word. "I'm not gay!" I shouted.

She stepped back and raised her hands in an I-come-in-peace gesture. "Well, I just wanted you to know that I didn't tell them about … ya know. I haven't told anyone."

I stared into the stream of water running from the tap over my hands. I didn't even flinch as the temperature rose to scalding. I was expecting her to turn and leave but as I looked up I could see in the mirror that she was still standing behind me.

"What is it that you want from me?"

It was her turn to shrug her shoulders.

I turned to face her and said, "I'm okay. Your conscience is clear, so enjoy the rest of your day."

She walked towards me and slowly held both of my wet hands squeezing them three times. Before I could register the act of kindness, her lips were softly bumping against mine.

I broke away in disbelief and stumbled into the sink. "Wh-what was that?" I spluttered.

She took my hand again and replied, "Sam, I miss you. I am so sorry for how I've treated you. I'm a bitch. I don't even like those stupid girls."

I stared at her, blinking furiously. The school bell rang out and disturbed the comedy of errors playing out in the girls' toilet. She let go of my hand, sighed deeply and gave me a warm but concerned smile. I wanted to say something but I had no words. She turned slowly and walked away, leaving me with only the running tap for company.

As I lay curled up on the floor in my bedroom that night, I could feel the pain inside my head while I retraced my day over and over in my mind. What was wrong with me and why did I always feel so sad? It felt like I was addicted to my own unhappiness. I simply couldn't break the cycle of feeling hopeless, no matter how hard I tried. It felt like an invisible weight sitting permanently on my chest that I could never be rid off no matter how much I punched myself. The dull throbbing of my headache and the self-inflicted punches to the temple made me feel in control. I was attacking the root of the pain by attacking the negative thoughts within. I thought if I kept hitting myself I could dislodge whatever it was that was making me feel so sad, as well as punish myself for being weak and unable to cope.

My schoolbag was on the other side of my room along with my blazer that I loathed wearing. The material was heavy and far too itchy when the weather was warm, but without it I would be condemned to a lifetime of lunchtime detention. I got up from the floor, picked up my bag and rummaged inside for my pencil case. It was covered in Tip-Ex pen and hilarious but highly immature drawings of a penis with ghastly overgrown pubic hair and droopy boobs, drawn in pen by my idiot mates. Flicking my fingers through pencil shavings, four erasers I never used and numerous pens that didn't work, I found what I was looking for – my compass. I took it out and stared at the sharp point for a while. Rolling up my left sleeve, I braced myself and closed my eyes. I laid the tip of the compass against the skin on the inside of my wrist and began to apply some pressure, inhaling and exhaling slowly to steady my breathing. I had begun to calmly count to three when my brother burst into the room. He was wailing about his missing shin pads for football training and demanding to know if I had seen them. I hadn't. I dropped the compass. I don't think he saw me.

Chapter Twenty-Three

Jason threw himself down onto the chair next to me, stinking of cigarettes but more fragrant than myself. He must've smoked at least two of them in succession while we all were inside. Owen made a display of coughing at the smell and picked up his green backpack.

"Well guys, this has been truly horrific and I need to head into the office and salvage what I can after going AWOL from work today."

With that he air-kissed us all and hugged me from behind. "Did you need me to pick up anything on my way home? We have milk, right?"

I smiled and nodded my head. "I've got it covered. I'll see you in a bit."

Sophie took Owen's lead and lifted herself out of the chair. "I just need some alone time, some chips and a decent therapist! Sam, get my number from Toni and make sure you guys use it. Toodles!"

She hesitated for a moment as if she wanted to embrace us all, but in true form, she composed herself, straightened her posture and left the bar without another word.

"I really should go with her," Toni said, necking the dregs of her drink. "And we need to sort out what happens to our flat now Uly is gone." She rose out of her chair and began to put on her jacket. Was she really just going to go without saying anything? She motioned towards the front door and I shouted out, in what can only be described as pure unadulterated desperation, "But how will I contact you?"

She turned and smiled with that same damn smile that had bewitched my senses to begin with. "You know where I work!" And with that she sashayed out the door.

Jason coughed with intent and grabbed my wrist, encouraging me to sit down and maintain whatever was left of my dignity.

"I know, I know," I said, reading Jason's face. "I'm a creature of habit who desires only things that will destroy me in the end."

And then there were two.

I looked over at the clock behind the bar – 11.45 p.m.

"Do you think Uly's death was painless and fairly quick?" Jason asked, maybe rhetorically.

I couldn't hold it in any longer. We needed to address the giant elephant in the room, wearing a feather boa and dancing to the *Macarena*. "Jason, what happened to your dad?"

He rubbed his forehead but didn't make eye contact with me. He was clearly uncomfortable but I wasn't going to let this go. The rules of our fun friendship didn't matter anymore, and this time there was no high-octane pop music to divert our attention and montage our way to the end of this debacle of a day.

Jason rubbed his forehead again but with more force this time. It looked painful. He then took a breath and began playing with the beer mat on the table. "I kept telling Dad to give my number to his mates for emergencies, but he always forgot. We would get ourselves into silly arguments about it every time I visited. The last time I was there, I left it written on a Post-It note stuck to the fridge door. But of course the silly bastard forgot again!" Jason smiled and I reached over the table to stop him from tearing the beer mat into even tinier pieces.

"He didn't show up for work two mornings ago, so his work mate called around to his house yesterday to check up on him. Nobody had my contact number, you see, so his friend had no choice but to call the police." Jason paused as his bottom lip began to tremble. He then looked down at the ground.

"He was found on the landing hanging from one of the beams in the ceiling. My mother always hated those damn beams but my dad thought they added character to the place."

My heart was aching at every word. I was expecting a heart attack or a stroke but not suicide.

Jason continued, "The selfish bastard decided to leave me just like my mother did. I knew he was in a bad way after she died, but he could've talked to me, ya know. Or maybe I should have made more of an effort to call him, let him know he wasn't the only person dealing with this miserable shitty world. I didn't want him to feel alone. So that's that. I have to sort out another fucking funeral. I guess I better get onto that today."

I couldn't muster any words. My eyes were stinging with tears and from blinking in an attempt to shove them back into their tear ducts. I didn't want to make this moment about me and my inability to hold myself together, so I figured silence and handholding was sufficient for now. Jason continued to stare at

117

the ground, shoulders drooped, beaten into submission by grief. He'd lost his mother to cancer just a year before, and now his dad too. He was an only child, so he had nobody else to lean on or who could understand the true extent of the heartbreak. Sympathy only goes so far. Unless I unzipped Jason and stepped into his skin, walked in his body and felt his pain, I could never appreciate what he was going through. Sure condolences are comforting, but "I'm sorry for your loss" could never give him what he really wanted.

"I failed him, Sam. I couldn't even save my own father from himself. And look at the past twenty-four hours! This was all my doing. It started right here with me and I landed us all in a police station! Not one good thing has come out of this, Sam, not one." Jason picked up his drink and swallowed. "I'm a fucking waster."

I shouted, "Stop it!" But Jason had every right to roll around in self-pity and blame himself, even though it wasn't his fault, and nobody had the right to tell him what to think or what to say. But I needed to tell him something. Something that was ripping a hole in me and I had no idea how to mend.

"Same again?" Jason asked, drinking the last of his pint.

I shook my head. He shrugged his shoulders and got up to go to the bar. It was my turn to grab his wrist and pull him back down.

"Your phone call last night saved my life, J." I shifted awkwardly in the chair from one bum cheek to the next. I hesitated, aware that I was about to make this hellish moment about me, but there would never be a moment like this again. So I just ploughed on, twirling my dead mobile phone in my right hand.

"I wasn't having a great evening yesterday. Well … I haven't really been having a great evening for months now. So I decided I would make a cup of tea, take a bath and then … urmm … well … down the entire contents of a packet of painkillers."

I could hear Jason shuffle his body around to face mine as I kept my eyes locked on the edge of my empty glass, petrified to meet his eye. Reliving yesterday was causing my stomach to churn, and the feelings of desperation and fear were now escaping my eyes and rolling down my cheeks. I quickly wiped the tears away and steadied my voice. Jason was probably waiting for the punch line but I still didn't dare look at him.

"I haven't been feeling great for some time now and I didn't know how to fix it. I'm having these, urmm, anxiety attacks everyday and I can't control the thoughts in my head. I just wanted to sleep. But then you called and thrust me into a mad adventure like you always do! Yes, it's been insane and yes I will probably be scarred for life, but seeing death with my own eyes and knowing what your father did has made me realise it's not what I want. I still have no real idea what it is I actually want, but I don't want to make my friends and family feel like you do right now. So you say nothing good has come from this, but I say you kept me going through a *force majeure*, and for that I am deeply indebted to you."

I finally looked up and it was Jason's turn to be silent. He leaned over and gently kissed my cheek. His stubble was scratchy but the kiss was very welcome.

"I like the way you talk," Jason said, meaning my delivery rather than the content. "So what do we do now?"

I looked up to the ceiling and deliberated for a second. "Well, you're going to come back to mine, we're going to get out of these clothes– "

"And finally have earth shattering sex?"

"No, Jason. Not sex." I rolled my eyes. "We are just gonna lie like vegetables for while. Then we're going to get onto these funeral arrangements and give your dad the best send off."

Jason smiled. I pushed my chair back to get up and leave.

"And you, Sam? What are you going to do?"

I was confused by his question at first, and then I realised I couldn't just drop a dark bombshell and leave it at that.

"Me? I'm going to look for a new job, see a doctor, speak to my mum, arrange to meet my friend Kai for an overdue drink. Oh, and stop falling for sexually ambiguous but super-hot women!" I guess it was time to change the things I hated and start doing the things I really loved before time ran out on me.

Jason nodded in approval and then suggested, "Maybe you should also stop expecting so much from life. Appreciate what you have now. That's often where our bullshit heartache begins – placing too much pressure on ourselves, giving in to delusions of grandeur, expecting to be somewhere else or someone different instead of accepting that we're just here in the present, still breathing and what will be will simply be."

I stopped to consider his existential thought for a moment before I said, "Fuck off, Yoda! Let's go home!"

Chapter Twenty-Four

I raised my body from the floor and heaved myself onto my futon. Owen hated this bed, so we'd swapped a few months ago and now he had mine and I had this. I liked the fact that it felt like I was in my own fort of pillows and duvets, camping out on the ground. As I lay on the bed I felt really weak and ashamed having spending the last fifteen minutes hitting myself in the head with my fist. It usually calmed me down but this time I felt like I had failed. I sighed, placed my oversized headphones over my ears and pressed play. Maybe it was music I needed to drown out the tinny reverb of my own thoughts. But it didn't work. When life was good, I could just enjoy music for what it was. On a superficial level it just made me feel happy. But when life was complicated, all I could hear were the lyrics as my brain tried to make out the intent of the words. I flung my headphones to the other side of the bed. Nothing was going to quell this panic and disgust clawing at my chest and I was too tired to let it continue. I just couldn't manage. It was time to admit defeat.

I shuffled out of my bed and walked to the bathroom. I opened the cabinet and pulled out the packet of painkillers I'd purchased a week and a half ago. It was a fresh packet, so I was okay. It should be enough. I closed the cabinet door and stared into the mirror. I loathed what I saw. My eyes seemed misty and my nose was bulbous and red. I was hideous and offensive on every level. I splashed some water on my face and then made my way to the kitchen. As I flicked on the kettle, I considered calling my mum for a chat, just to say hello, ask her about her day and tell her I loved her. People don't say that enough. Three silly words that are thrown around like dust but rarely said for the best reason of all – just because. I loved her so much, even though I knew she saw a part of me as soiled. There was something broken that could only be fixed by pretending it didn't exist.

The whistle of Owen's vintage kettle, picked up at a flea market, soothed me back to the present. I walked over to the fridge and opened it. I should have known he'd forget. I would buy the milk myself.

Made in the USA
Charleston, SC
28 February 2015